GET ALL THIS FREE

WITH JUST ONE PROOF OF PURCHASE:

$50 VALUE

◆ **Hotel Discounts** up to 60% at home and abroad ◆ **Travel Service -** Guaranteed lowest published airfares plus 5% cash back on tickets ◆ **$25 Travel Voucher** ◆ **Sensuous Petite Parfumerie** collection ◆ **Insider Tips Letter** with sneak previews of upcoming books

You'll get a FREE personal card, too. It's your passport to all these benefits—and to even more great gifts & benefits to come!

There's no club to join. No purchase commitment. No obligation.

HT-PP5A

Enrollment Form

☐ *Yes!* I WANT TO BE A *P*RIVILEGED *W*OMAN.
Enclosed is one *PAGES & PRIVILEGES*™ Proof of
Purchase from any Harlequin or Silhouette book currently for
sale in stores (Proofs of Purchase are found on the back pages
of books) and the store cash register receipt. Please enroll me
in *PAGES & PRIVILEGES*™. Send my Welcome Kit and FREE
Gifts -- and activate my FREE benefits -- immediately.

More great gifts and benefits to come.

► DETACH HERE AND MAIL TODAY! ►

NAME (please print)
_____

ADDRESS   **APT. NO**
_____

CITY   **STATE**   **ZIP/POSTAL CODE**

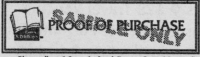

PROOF OF PURCHASE ONLY

NO CLUB!
NO COMMITMENT!
Just one purchase brings
you great Free Gifts and
Benefits!

Please allow 6-8 weeks for delivery. Quantities are limited. We reserve the right to
substitute items. Enroll before October 31, 1995 and receive one full year of benefits.

Name of store where this book was purchased_____

Date of purchase_____

Type of store:

    ☐ Bookstore   ☐ Supermarket   ☐ Drugstore
    ☐ Dept. or discount store (e.g. K-Mart or Walmart)
    ☐ Other (specify)_____

Which Harlequin or Silhouette series do you usually read?
_____

Complete and mail with one Proof of Purchase and store receipt to:
U.S.: *PAGES & PRIVILEGES*™, P.O. Box 1960, Danbury, CT 06813-1960
Canada: *PAGES & PRIVILEGES*™, 49-6A The Donway West, P.O. 813,
      North York, ON M3C 2E8

HT-PP5B

"Take off your belt and unbutton your jeans."

T.R. complied, his eyes daring her not to look away. As Freddy watched, she cursed her decision to take him out on the trail.

"I'm ready." His jeans were unfastened and his hands were braced on either side of him in what seemed to be an unconscious gesture of invitation. "Got a bullet for me to bite down on?"

"You've seen too many movies." Taking a deep breath, she tugged off the stiff denim. In spite of her efforts not to touch him, her fingers encountered firm muscle and the tantalizing brush of hair. She swallowed and wrenched the jeans over his feet with more force than was necessary. He gasped, but didn't cry out.

"There." With a sigh of relief, Freddy got to her feet. But her relief was short-lived. She watched as T.R. took some liniment from the tin and began dabbing it over the inside of his thighs.

"Not like that," she said before she could stop herself.

"You want to show me how?" he said softly.

Dear Reader,

Welcome to the True Love Ranch! And before you scoff and assume a *real* ranch would never have such a name, let me assure you it's entirely possible. While I was researching old ranches and brands for this series, I discovered that cowboys are a sentimental lot. Unless you've studied old brands, you might be surprised at the number of them that incorporate hearts and even flowers! Out in the West, a man treasured a good woman, and although he sometimes had trouble putting his devotion into words, he could say it with something far more important to him—his official brand.

That sort of touching gesture may be at the root of our continued love affair with cowboys. They work hard at presenting a tough-as-rawhide exterior, yet never quite disguise a heart warmer than a campfire and passion hotter than a branding iron.

Most men have a little bit of cowboy in them, but the three men in the Urban Cowboys series have a lot. Although they were raised in the city, T.R., Chase and Joe can't become the men they were destined to be until they head out West. I hope you have as much fun as I did watching three city slickers become transformed into bronc-ridin', rope-slingin', fast-lovin' cowboys.

Happy trails,

Vicki Lewis Thompson

Vicki Lewis Thompson
THE TRAILBLAZER

Harlequin Books

TORONTO • NEW YORK • LONDON
AMSTERDAM • PARIS • SYDNEY • HAMBURG
STOCKHOLM • ATHENS • TOKYO • MILAN
MADRID • WARSAW • BUDAPEST • AUCKLAND

For David Santa Maria,
who helped me build the True Love Ranch

ISBN 0-373-25655-8

THE TRAILBLAZER

Prologue

JUST BEFORE the elevator reversed direction and plummeted to the basement, T. R. McGuinnes was thinking about going West. Golden opportunities awaited bold investors who could foresee the direction of growth in the Sun Belt and buy land in its path. As a commodities trader, T.R. prided himself on boldness, but he needed partners. Partners with cash.

Without warning, a relay failed between the second and third floors, catapulting the elevator toward the bottom at a thousand feet per minute. T.R. had approximately three seconds to review his life and wish he'd scheduled his business appointments differently that morning. He looked around and met the startled gazes of the two men who shared the elevator with him, one in jeans, the other in NYPD blues. The man in jeans swore once, loudly, just before the elevator slammed into its concrete base. T.R. was tossed against the elevator wall, cracked his head on the handrail coming down and blacked out.

1

THE GROAN of stressed metal eased into T.R.'s consciousness. He opened his eyes to blackness, breathed in dust and coughed.

"Who's that?" rasped a voice from the back of the elevator.

"Name's McGuinnes." His head pounded. "T. R. McGuinnes. You?"

"Chase Lavette. Are you the cop?"

"No."

"Do you think he's dead?"

"I hope to God he's not," T.R. said. "Are you hurt?"

"Yeah. Something's wrong with my back. It hurts like hell. How about you?"

"I hit my head." T.R. put a hand to the side of his head, but he didn't feel blood, just the jackhammer pain. "Listen, you'd better not move," he said. "I'll check the cop." He got to his hands and knees, wincing at the viselike pressure against his skull. Crawling forward, he brushed something with his shoulder. He reached up and touched the warm surface of a fluorescent light that had been knocked from the ceiling.

"It's getting damned hot in here," Lavette said.

"Yeah." Perspiration soaked his shirt, but it wasn't only the heat making him sweat. It was the thought that he could be approaching a corpse.

"They should be coming to get us out of here pretty soon," Lavette told him.

"Let's hope so." A pinpoint of light from the damaged ceiling allowed T.R. to make out a shapeless mass near the left side of the elevator doors. As he crept toward the body, his knee hit the edge of his briefcase and he wondered if his briefcase, flying through the air, could kill a man. The smell of blood made his gorge rise.

When he reached the cop, he forced himself to place two fingers against the guy's neck. It was wet and he couldn't feel a pulse. Oh, God. He leaned closer. *Breathe, damn you.*

"If you try mouth-to-mouth resuscitation, you're a dead man," the cop said wearily.

T.R.'s breath whooshed out in relief. "Never learned it, anyway." He sat on his heels and reached in his back pocket for a handkerchief to wipe the blood from his hands. Then he shoved the handkerchief toward the cop. "Here. You're bleeding somewhere."

"No joke. How's the other guy?"

"I'll survive," Lavette said.

"Says his back hurts," T.R. added. "I told him not to move."

"Good. Moving a back injury case and severing his spinal cord would top off this episode nicely." The cop eased himself up to a sitting position and winced as he touched the handkerchief to his face. "That briefcase cut the hell out of my chin. What's that thing made of, steel?"

"Brass trim."

The cop snorted. "You got a cellular phone in it, at least?"

"Yeah."

"Then you'd better use it. This has been great fun, but I'm due back at the station in an hour."

T.R. groped behind him for his briefcase. "I suppose almost getting killed is a big yawner for you, isn't it?"

"Killed in an elevator accident? You've been seeing too many Keanu Reeves movies. New York elevators are safer than your grandmother's rocking chair."

"Tell that to my back," Lavette said. "I can't drive with a busted back, and if I can't drive, I can't pay off my rig."

T.R. opened his briefcase, found his cellular phone and snapped it open. "If you can't drive, you'll get an insurance settlement."

"And sit around doing nothing? No, thanks."

T.R. dialed 911, gave their location and problem and hit the Disconnect button. "They're sending a team to get us out," he said. As the news penetrated his numb brain, an adrenaline rush hit his system and he almost dropped the phone. He clenched his fist around it and fought the trembling just as the elevator rumbled and lurched to the right.

"Damn!" Lavette cried out. "Aren't we all the way down yet?"

"We're all the way down," the cop said. "The blasted thing's still settling, that's all. Move your fingers and toes, see if you still have all your motor coordination."

Paralysis. The thought sickened T.R.

Lavette rustled around a little. "I can move everything," he said at last and T.R. sagged with the sudden release of tension.

"Good," said the cop. "What's your name?"

"Lavette. Chase Lavette."

"T. R. McGuinnes," T.R. said, taking his cue.

"Joe Gilardini," the cop supplied. "I wish I could say it was nice to meet you guys, but under the circumstances, I wish I'd been denied the pleasure."

"Same here," Lavette said.

Sweat dripped down T.R.'s chin and he wiped it with the sleeve of his suit jacket. What they all needed was a distraction, he decided. He scrambled for ideas and came up with the last topic that had occupied his mind before the elevator had crashed. "Either one of you ever been out West?"

"Why do you want to know?" Lavette asked.

"I don't, really. I just think talking is better than sitting here waiting for the elevator to shift again."

"Guess you're right," Lavette said. "No, I've never been out West. Eastern seaboard's my route. Always wanted to go out there, though."

The cop sighed. "God, so have I. The wide-open spaces. Peace and quiet."

"No elevators," Lavette put in.

"Yeah," Gilardini said. "If I didn't have my kid living in New York, I'd turn in my badge, collect my pension and go."

T.R. thought he should probably be locked up for the way his mind was working all of a sudden. Only a crazy person would start putting together a business deal at the bottom of an elevator shaft with his fellow crash victims. Or maybe not so crazy. He'd just been reminded that life is short, and you'd better grab what you can, when you can. A pension and an insurance settlement. It might be enough, with what he could raise. Of course, these guys probably didn't know the first thing about investing, but maybe that was what he needed. His usual contacts knew so much, they'd turned gun-shy on him.

"I just heard about this guest ranch in Arizona that's up for sale," he said. "One of those working guest ranches with a small herd of cattle. I'm going out there next week to look it over."

"No kidding?" Lavette said. "Think you might buy it?"

"If it checks out."

"Running a guest ranch," Gilardini mused aloud. "You know, that wouldn't be half-bad."

"And after I've had some fun with it, I'll sell it for a nice profit," T.R. said, sweetening the deal. "Tucson's growing in that direction, and in a couple of years developers will be crying out to get their hands on that land, all one hundred and sixty acres of it. I can't lose."

"A hundred and sixty acres," Lavette said with reverence.

"I'm looking for partners."

The cop laughed. "Now I've heard everything. Only in New York would a guy use an accident as a chance to set up a deal."

The elevator settled with another metallic groan.

"Would you rather sit here and think about the elevator collapsing on us?" T.R. asked.

"I'd rather think about your ranch," Lavette said. "I'd go in on it in a minute if I had the cash."

"You might get that settlement," T.R. reminded him.

"You know, I might," Lavette said. "Listen, McGuinnes, after we get out of here, let's keep in touch. You never know."

"I guarantee you wouldn't go wrong on this investment. The Sun Belt's booming."

"I think you're both nut cases," Gilardini said.

"So you're not interested?" T.R. asked.

"I didn't say that. Hell, what else is there to be interested in down in this hole? If the ranch looks good, just call the Forty-third Precinct and leave a message for me."

T.R. shook his hand. "Let me get some business cards out of my briefcase."

"I'd just as soon not think about your briefcase, McGuinnes. Let's talk some more about the ranch. What's the name of it, anyway? I always liked those old ranch names—the Bar X, the Rocking J. Remember "Bonanza"?"

"I saw that on reruns," Lavette said. "The guy I liked was Clint Eastwood. I snuck in to see *High Plains Drifter* at least six times when I was a kid. Back then, I would have given anything to be a cowboy."

"Yeah, me too," admitted the cop. "So what's the place called?"

T.R. hesitated. These guys were after macho images, and he wished he could give them one. "Well, this spread is named something a little different."

"Yeah?" Gilardini said. "What could be so different?"

"The True Love Ranch."

FREDDY SINGLETON hung up the phone and glared at her younger sister, Leigh, who was perched on the edge of the old pine desk. "Damn. That was Janine at Cooper Realty and she wants us to send the van for that T. R. McGuinnes from New York."

"Do we have to?"

Freddy shrugged. "I'll catch hell from the Westridge corporate types if I don't. They want us to roll out the red carpet for him. They think he's got money. Shoot. I was hoping he wasn't serious. Then maybe Eb's offer would stand."

"Fat chance," Leigh said. "Westridge wants at least their original investment back." She pushed away from the desk and walked over to study the gallery of framed photographs displayed on the office walls. "Maybe they're hoping for a bidding war between Eb and this Easterner."

"Eb can't go any higher." Freddy tapped a pencil against the desk in frustration. "Just what we need, a greenhorn trying to run the place. Eb Whitlock would just leave me alone to do my thing."

Leigh turned back to her. "Maybe the guy won't be interested once he sees the ranch. We *are* looking a little shabby in spots. And we're low on guests this week. What have we got, eleven? That won't seem like a money-making operation."

"Here's a clue for you, Leigh. It isn't. I've never seen it so slow in May."

"So we'll convert our weaknesses to strengths. Maybe we can scare him off. Don't forget to tell him about the old Indian curse that's supposed to hang over this property."

"Yeah, Westridge has been on my case about all the little mishaps we've had lately. Sometimes I wonder if there really is a curse." Freddy dialed the bunkhouse and asked Duane to make an airport run, then hung up and glanced up at Leigh. "We might as well go down to the corrals and get this morning's chore over with. Are you ready to convince Red Devil that sex isn't all it's cracked up to be?"

Leigh chuckled. "I don't think there's a male animal alive who would accept castration with grace, but I'll do what I can. After all, that's what a head wrangler gets paid for."

Freddy stood and reached for her hat hanging from a peg on the wall. "You know, I wonder if we really could discourage this T.R. person from buying the ranch."

"He's a dude, right?" Leigh said. "We have ways of handling dudes."

"That we do." Freddy adjusted her hat so the brim settled low over her eyes. "And I'd do just about anything to get rid of this particular tenderfoot."

T.R. WASN'T SURPRISED when the guest ranch van that met him at the airport had steer horns on the hood instead of a standard hood ornament. With a ranch named the True Love, he was lucky the ornament wasn't a valentine heart.

Despite the air-conditioning, it was hot inside the van. He took off his sport coat, making sure Joe Gilardini's home phone number was still tucked in the pocket. He and Joe had been released from the hospital emergency room the same day as the accident, Joe with a broken arm as well as the nasty cut on his chin, and T.R. with a mild concussion. Lavette was still in the hospital with lower back pain and no clear predictions from the doctors on whether he could resume his trucking career, but he was more eager to get in on the ranch deal than Gilardini.

The driver of the van was a certified cowboy named Duane, grizzled and taciturn. His sun-weathered skin made judging his age difficult, but he was probably about forty-five. T.R. gave up on conversation after a few monosyllabic responses from the man and watched Duane navigate the heavy city traffic of Tucson. It wasn't hard to picture him guiding a cutting horse through a restless herd of cattle with the same dedication.

T.R. glanced out the window and grinned. He might be on a freeway, but there was no doubt he was in the West. Mountains surrounded the city, but the Santa Catalinas dominated it. It wasn't a gentle range.

As they drove, civilization loosened its grip on the landscape and T.R. gazed at hillsides covered with giant saguaros standing fifty- to sixty-feet high, their massive arms lifted toward a sky so blue T.R. took off his sunglasses to make sure the color wasn't an optical trick. It wasn't.

The van turned off the main road where two battered rural mailboxes crouched, one marked Singleton in faded letters, and the other Whitlock. Near the boxes was a small white sign that read True Love Guest Ranch—2 miles. Beneath the lettering was a heart with an arrow through it. T.R. could imagine what Joe would say about that. He had to convince the cop that none of that mattered. The name and the corny heart would disappear in a couple of years, anyway. They could even change the name immediately if Joe insisted on something more . . . manly.

The van jolted along a dirt road that needed grading, sending a plume of dust behind it. A lane branched off to the right, and a wooden sign announced a turnoff to the Rocking W Ranch—Whitlock's property, T.R. concluded. Several yards down the lane, a gaunt figure in a battered straw cowboy hat supported himself with an aluminum walker as he inched along in the direction of the ranch house. A plastic shopping bag filled with mail hung on one side of the walker.

"Who's that?" T.R. asked Duane.

"Dexter."

As the van drew alongside, Dexter turned slowly and lifted one hand in a salute. Duane raised two fingers from the steering wheel and drove past.

"Aren't you going to give him a ride?"

"Nope."

"Why not?"

"I don't aim to insult Dex."

T.R. glanced back at the old cowboy shuffling along the dirt road. "He picks up the mail every day?"

Duane shifted his tobacco to the other side of his lip. "Yep."

"How long does it take him?"

"Good days, an hour."

T.R. settled in the seat and tried not to think about Dexter's daily trek to the mailbox. It was too personal, too human—the sort of information he'd rather not know, considering his plans for the True Love.

The road forked again, and another sign appeared which read Main House—Registration, and pointed to the right. Beneath that was the word *corrals* and another arrow, this one pointing to the left. And below all that, the darned heart with an arrow through it. These people weren't shy about their sentimentality.

Duane slowed the van at the fork. "Freddy's down at the corrals. I should probably take you there first."

T.R. was impressed that Duane was capable of making such a long speech. "Fine," he agreed. He had to see all of it, so it didn't much matter which end he started with. "What's going on at the corrals?" he asked, not really expecting an explanation.

"Last I heard, Freddy was fixin' to use the emasculator on Red Devil."

T.R. swallowed. From the corner of his eye, he could see Duane watching him for a reaction. He'd never heard of an emasculator, but it didn't take much imagination to figure out what was in store for Red Devil. He adopted the poker face that had served him so well as a deal maker. "Sounds interesting," he said evenly. "Maybe I'll be in time to watch."

"Maybe you will," Duane said, a slow grin spreading across his leathered face as he took the left fork in the road.

T.R. prayed the corrals were a long, long way down this winding road, and that Freddy had already finished the task.

Shortly, however, the corrals appeared. They didn't look very much like the ones T.R. had seen in the movies. The fences were at least a foot thick and made with tree branches laid lengthwise inside upright braces to form a solid wall. The weathered nature of the branches indicated the corrals had been there a long time. One large enclosure containing at least thirty horses was surrounded by several smaller corrals, which were empty. Not far from the corrals stood a large tin barn with two wings, one of tin, and one of stone, looking much older than its counterpart. Across a small clearing was a long one-story building, also of stone, that looked as though it might be a bunkhouse.

A group of cowboys clustered around one of the small corrals. Laughter wafted across the clearing, as if the men were at a party.

"I'll park here, so we don't get no dust over there," Duane said. "Come on," he urged, climbing down from the driver's seat. "We'll get a little closer so you can see."

T.R. took a deep breath and loosened his tie. "Okay." He left his sport coat in the van, deciding a jacket wasn't required at this particular event. Following Duane, he trudged through dust that coated his oxblood wing tips. It sure didn't smell like the city, he thought. But he sort of liked the combined odor of horse manure and animal sweat that hung over the area.

Duane paused next to the fence and found a foothold in the meshed branches. "Just climb up here. You can see, then."

T.R. put his hands on the rough bark, wedged his wing tips in a notch in the branches and hoisted himself up next to Duane. Inside the small corral where the cowboys had gathered, a cinnamon-colored horse lay on the ground, his back leg stretched away from his body with a rope.

A blond woman crouched near the horse's head, and a brunette was kneeling by his groin area. T.R. had a sudden uneasy suspicion. "Where's Freddy?" he asked.

"Right there by the business end of the horse. The blonde is Leigh, her sister. She's the head wrangler."

"Oh." He hated surprises. They threw him off his stride.

Duane looked at him. "Freddy's the best boss I ever slung a rope for, mister. And a damned good vet. She took it in school, just so's she could help out with animals around here."

"I'm sure she's very capable," T.R.'s mind raced to assimilate this unexpected information. Freddy had her back to him, her snug-fitting jeans cupping a firm backside, her leather belt cinching in a small waist. Her rich brunette hair was caught with a silver-and-turquoise clip at her nape.

"Leigh calls herself a horse psychic," Duane said. "Some folks laugh about it, but I've known people who could tell what horses are thinkin'. Seems like Leigh can. She's gonna work on Red Devil's self-esteem, I think is what she said."

After that speech, T.R. realized that Duane wasn't quiet at all. Probably, he just got that way in the unfriendly confines of the city. Out here on the ranch, conversation spewed from him like water from a broken fire hydrant.

But most of T.R.'s attention remained focused on Freddy. Her cooperation would be critical once the purchase went through, because he wanted to continue the guest ranch operation without sinking any more money into improvements. It would be a waste of resources, considering the ultimate fate of the property.

Freddy turned and asked for something and T.R. got a glimpse of her profile. Classic. So she had a face to match her figure, apparently. Now that he'd adjusted to the idea that the ranch foreman was a woman, he liked it. Women were just as good working companions as men. Who knew if Freddy might turn out to be more reasonable about his plans for the ranch than some macho guy protecting his turf. Sometimes women were better at the art of compromise.

"They've sedated him, but they ain't done the cuttin' yet," Duane said, as if he felt obliged to provide color commentary on the event. "Ever seen anythin' like this before?"

"No." T.R. wondered if this was the way Elizabethans used to react to beheadings in the public square—too horrified to watch and too curious to look away. He winced as Freddy began the procedure and fought the urge to put his hands over his own crotch.

"That there's the emasculator," Duane explained, pointing to an instrument in Freddy's hands. "Looks sorta like a nutcracker, don't it? No pun intended."

T.R. wanted to turn his back on the whole thing, but he figured this might be a test, and for some stupid reason, he didn't want Duane to think less of him.

As the operation continued, Duane shifted his weight uneasily. So he wasn't as unperturbed about this as he let on, T.R. thought. "Kinda gets you in the—well, you know," the cowboy said.

"Yeah, I know," T.R. said. He found it interesting that Duane seemed reluctant to mention body parts. He'd heard that cowboys had a chivalrous side and avoided many of the four-letter words tossed out so often by city dwellers. Some of T.R.'s Wall Street friends might laugh at the idea that a tobacco-spitting old cowpoke was a gentleman, but that's exactly how T.R. would describe Duane.

At last, Freddy stood, signaling that the operation was over. T.R. realized his jaw hurt, and he relaxed his clenched teeth.

Duane climbed down. "That does it. Might as well take you over to meet the boss. Walk careful and don't stir up no dust. We don't want any on Red Devil's ... equipment."

T.R. eased himself off the fence, wiped his sweaty palms on his slacks and started after Duane. As they approached, the blond sister named Leigh noticed them and spoke to Freddy.

The ranch foreman turned and stripped off her gloves. Striding toward them, she held out her hand to T.R. "Welcome to the True Love, Mr. McGuinnes. I'm Frederica Singleton. Please call me Freddy."

T.R. looked into hazel eyes that assessed him with calm intelligence. Her grip was firm, although her skin was temptingly soft. He reminded himself these were the same hands that had just turned a stallion into a gelding. He'd be wise not to underestimate Freddy Singleton.

2

HE HAS New York written all over him, Freddy thought as she took in the pallor of his skin from being indoors too much, the sophisticated cut of his thick brown hair, the bold red-and-blue stripes of his power tie. But his blue-eyed gaze was direct, his smile friendly, even a little sexy. She almost regretted what she was about to do to him. Almost.

"I understand you want to inspect the ranch," she said.

"That's right."

"The best way to see the True Love is from the back of a horse. Can you ride?"

"Yes."

She could just imagine. A little tour around Central Park on a Sunday afternoon, perhaps. But she was glad he'd likely done that much. If he'd never ridden at all, she'd have a tougher time instituting her plan. She surveyed his pristine white shirt and gray herringbone slacks and tried to keep the smile from her voice. "Did you bring anything besides that sort of outfit?"

"No."

Freddy had already anticipated this problem. She dismissed Duane as being too short, but Curtis, who was mending a fence a few yards away, was about T.R.'s height and build. She called him over. "Think you have a pair of jeans and a long-sleeved shirt you could loan our guest? We're going to take a ride around the ranch."

"Around the ranch?" Curtis blinked.

"Yes."

Curtis pushed back his hat and studied T.R. with new interest. "I reckon I have somethin'. What about boots?"

"Listen," T.R. said, "I don't think I should inconvenience—"

"No problem," Freddy interrupted. "What size shoe do you wear?"

"Eleven."

Freddy lifted an eyebrow in Curtis's direction.

He shook his head. "Tens."

"I wear an eleven," Duane said, bending down to pull off one scuffed boot. With no apparent reluctance, he put his sock foot—with a large hole in the toe—on the ground and held the boot out toward T.R. "Try this."

Freddy loved it. She'd bet no one had ever shoved used footwear in T. R. McGuinnes's face, let alone expected him to put it on. He might not realize what a huge favor Duane was granting him, but he was obviously a polite guy. His natural big-city reticence carved grooves beside his mouth as he seemed to be struggling for a graceful way out of taking off his expensive wing tips and trying on the boot. He must have come up empty, because he accepted the boot, walked over to the fence and propped a foot against the rail to untie his shoe.

Freddy considered suggesting that if the boot fit, T.R. could just trade Duane the boots for the wing tips for a few days, but she decided that might be going a bit far. Besides, Duane wouldn't be caught dead in city shoes like that, not even for a joke.

Duane spat a stream of tobacco in the dirt. "My folks always said I woulda been taller if God hadn't turned up so much for feet," he said with a tobacco-stained grin. "You know he's gonna need a hat," he added in a lower voice. "I'm willin' to loan out my boots 'cause I got the others back at the bunkhouse, but I ain't givin' up my hat, and I don't know any of the hands who would."

"Don't worry. We'll find something in that collection we keep for the dudes who don't remember to bring their own."

Duane made a face. "A man's gotta have a decent hat."

"Only if he decides to stay," Freddy answered with a wink.

T.R. returned wearing Duane's boot on one foot, his pant leg tucked inside, and his dusty wing tip on the other. "They fit fine, but I really think—"

"Perfect," Freddy said, motioning for Duane to take off his other boot.

He complied and held the second boot out to T.R. Then he turned back to Freddy. "Curtis and I can go on up to the bunkhouse, pick up Curtis's clothes for Mr. McGuinnes, here, and meet you at the ranch house in a few minutes."

"Sounds good." Freddy glanced back to where Leigh was standing guard over Red Devil until he came out of the anesthesia. "Let me make sure our patient is okay, Duane. Then I'll bring Mr. McGuinnes up to the house in my truck."

Duane looked at T.R., who was still holding the second boot. "Might as well put 'em both on. You look kinda discombobulated like that."

"All right."

As Freddy watched him return to the rail to take off his other shoe, she felt another twinge of conscience. But how else was she supposed to save the ranch from this Easterner if she didn't make him so miserable, he would never want to even *think* about a guest ranch in Arizona? The market was down, so maybe Eb Whitlock could buy the True Love, and life could go on undisturbed.

She walked back toward Leigh, careful not to stir up any dust. In a few days, Red Devil would be ready for use as a saddle horse again, and a much milder-tempered saddle horse he'd be, too.

She squatted next to Leigh, who was stroking Red Devil's neck and murmuring to him. "How's he taking it?" Freddy asked.

"He's still in dreamland. I'm picking up something about a little palomino filly."

"From now on, dreaming's all he'll be doing about that particular activity."

Leigh glanced at her and angled her head toward T.R., who was pulling on Duane's other boot. "So why's Duane giving up his boots?"

"Mr. McGuinnes needs something to ride in if he's going to survey the ranch."

Leigh's eyes widened. "All the ranch?"

"Sure. I figure we'll take a little ride around the perimeter, ending with a trip up Rogue Canyon into the leased Forest Service land, so he can see where we summer the herd."

A slow smile tilted the corners of Leigh's mouth. "That's a mighty long ride."

"I know."

"I doubt you could even finish it today."

"Precisely."

"And unless he's spent a lot of time on a horse..."

Freddy reached down and stroked Red Devil's velvet neck. "Do you think I'm being too cruel?"

"Not if you want to get rid of him."

"I do. And not just for our sakes, either. Belinda and Dexter are too old to deal with an Easterner, and Duane doesn't say much, but I can tell he's worried about keeping his job. Losing it would be the end of the world for him."

"It would," Leigh agreed. "You have to do it, Freddy. But maybe you should take some horse liniment. You don't want to have to call Search and Rescue to haul him out of the canyon."

"Great idea. If he's like most dudes, he'll hate the smell of the stuff, which will suit my purpose nicely. So, can you handle things until tomorrow?"

"Yeah, but you could be back sooner, depending on how much of a wimp this guy is."

Freddy thought of McGuinnes's firm handshake and his clear blue gaze. "No, I think we'll be out there for the duration. He may be in pain, but he'll tough it out."

"Sounds like he might not deserve his fate."

"He probably doesn't," Freddy acknowledged. "If I could think of any other way to keep him from buying the ranch, I'd do that, instead." She gave Red Devil one final pat. "See you tomorrow, big guy."

T.R. FINISHED PULLING on the second boot, took off his tie and tucked it into one of his shoes. Duane and Curtis left, and he hoped Duane remembered the sport coat in the van. Not that he was worried. A guy who would give you the boots off his feet wasn't about to steal a jacket. He chuckled, trying to imagine Duane wearing the navy blazer, even if he did make off with it. Duane would probably sooner be caught in a dress.

Freddy came toward him. "Ready?"

"Sure. How's Red Devil doing?"

"Leigh says he's dreaming of fillies."

"Poor guy."

Freddy smiled at him. "Unless we're planning to stand them at stud, stallions are a liability at a guest ranch. They're either after the mares or trying to pick a fight, which makes them too unpredictable for a guest to ride. The hands don't much like putting up with their shenanigans, either. Around here, we refer to gelding as brain surgery."

"Oh." He tried to appreciate the operation from a business standpoint and failed.

"Let's go," she said. "My truck's under the mesquite tree over there."

T.R. looked at the battered white pickup with the ranch brand stenciled on the door panel. Didn't seem like anyone was wasting money around here. He liked that. "What did you call this kind of tree?" he asked as they walked toward the truck.

"Mesquite."

He surveyed the stand of mesquite, gnarled trunks branching out into a canopy bursting with small, delicate leaves. "Do you sell the wood to restaurants back East? Mesquite-grilled meat is very popular where I come from."

Her glance was not friendly. "No, we don't sell the wood."

"Why not?" he persisted. "Seems like you have a lot of it around."

"The trees protect our privacy. My ancestors used to clear the mesquite to give the cattle more room, but a lot of our guests are birders, and the mesquite bosques attract birds. Besides, I don't much like the sound of a chain saw. It frightens the horses."

"I see." So economics wasn't her top priority, after all. T.R.'s hope that a woman would be more willing to compromise on his plans for the ranch began to disappear. Once the developers finished with this land, there wouldn't be a mesquite bosque to be found.

They reached the truck and he climbed in, dumping his shoes on the floor.

"How are the boots?" Freddy asked as she started the engine.

"Great fit." He'd discovered he liked the boots. With only one on, he'd felt stupid, but with both on, and his pant leg pulled over the shaft instead of tucked in, he felt like a cowboy. He'd always made fun of city people who wore Western clothing as a style statement. But something had happened when he'd put on the boots. He'd walked with more purpose in his stride and had felt more in command of his world. Maybe he'd take a taxi into town and buy some before he left.

Freddy steered the truck past the fork and down the road toward the main house.

"Your ancestors built this place?" T.R. asked, remembering something she'd said earlier.

"That's right. Thaddeus Singleton homesteaded the True Love in 1882." After a moment of silence, she continued, "And if you wonder why a Singleton is now only the foreman, and not the owner, after my dad died, I ran into some financial problems and had to sell. The Westridge Corporation out of Denver bought it. Fortunately, I was allowed to stay on and run the place."

"Considering what you must save them on vet bills alone, I'm sure the corporation is lucky you decided to stay."

She glanced at him, her smile grim. "I'd have to be dragged off the True Love."

He didn't like the sound of that, didn't like it at all. But she was obviously a very intelligent woman. Maybe, as time went by, he'd be able to appeal to her business sense.

The True Love property was too valuable to use as a guest ranch. Surely there was other land out in the middle of nowhere that could be had for a pittance. She needed to take a page out of Thaddeus Singleton's book and strike out on her own, carve a new ranch out of some remote wilderness. Maybe he could help her locate that piece of property, give her a business loan to start a new spread. The more he thought about it, the more he liked the idea of being her financial adviser.

The dirt road curved and the main house appeared, surrounded by a low wall of whitewashed adobe that swooped into an arch over a flagstone walk. A border of blue, white and yellow Mexican tile decorated the archway. Cactus that reminded T.R. of giant artichokes stood on either side of the arch, and beyond the wall two large mesquite trees created a filigree of shade over a yard with patchy grass. T.R. noticed a couple of rabbits munching on the grass and wondered how golf courses handled the rabbit situation.

"Here we are." Freddy parked the truck and swung to the ground. "The old ranch house, which was frame, burned down in the thirties, so my grandfather decided to build the new one of adobe—less of a fire hazard. It's grown like topsy over the years, but we've tried to keep Grandpa's basic design." She gestured toward the house. "You're standing at the base of a U shape. Sixteen guest rooms are on the right wing, living and dining room in the middle, and kitchen, storage and family areas on the left. Oh, and we have one little cottage about fifty yards away in a mesquite grove. We use it for honeymooners."

T.R. surveyed the one-story structure that stretched in front of him. *Graceful* was the word that came to him. A developer might want to convert the building into a clubhouse for the golf course because of its charm. The

whitewashed adobe contrasted nicely with the red
Spanish-tile roof, and a wide porch stretched the length
of the building, with potted geraniums blooming under
the porch's shade. Shade had quickly become important to T.R., whose shirt was already sticking to his back.
He noticed that Freddy seemed barely to perspire.

"Do you have many guests now?"

"Not many this week," she said. "A group of German
tourists will arrive on Sunday. The Europeans don't seem
to mind the heat, but the bulk of our business is during
the winter months, although business hasn't been that
terrific recently. Anyway, now's the time we catch up on
our chores."

Like castrating poor Red Devil, T.R. thought.

"Let's go in." She started down the flagstone walk, her
boot heels clicking on the hard surface. "Duane and
Curtis will be along in a minute with your luggage and
some riding clothes. In the meantime, I think Belinda can
find us each a glass of lemonade."

The suggestion reminded T.R. that he was desper-
ately thirsty. He never remembered being so thirsty in his
life.

Freddy grasped the wrought-iron handle set into one
of the carved wooden entry doors, opened the door and
ushered him inside. He nearly sighed with relief as cool
air welcomed him.

She led him through a short tiled hallway into a large
room with beamed ceilings at least fifteen feet high. In
the far left corner stood a huge beehive fireplace flanked
by worn leather couches and two leather easy chairs, also
battered. A rough pine coffee table held pewter ashtrays
and some back issues of *Arizona Highways.*

Next to the fireplace, a wide bay window looked out
on an enclosed courtyard, a kidney-shaped swimming

pool and a Jacuzzi. A high rock wall broken by an arch-way curved beside the pool, and a waterfall spilled from the top of the arch. A mother and her two young children played in the tumbling water. T.R.'s thirst grew.

"Why, there you are, Freddy," called a musical voice.

T.R. turned as a woman he judged to be in her mid-seventies walked into the room. Her gray hair was cut short in a no-nonsense style and she wore slacks and a flowered smock over her ample bosom. She had one of the sweetest faces he'd ever seen.

"You must be a mind reader, Belinda. We could sure use some lemonade." Freddy took off her hat and slapped it against her thigh. "But first, let me introduce you. Belinda Grimes, meet T. R. McGuinnes."

Belinda nodded to him politely, but without enthusiasm.

"When the True Love was strictly a working ranch, Belinda was the only cook, but now she supervises a staff of three," Freddy said. "She's been working here for fifty-one years."

"Fifty-two," Belinda corrected in her lilting voice. "I came in March and it's already May."

T.R. received the news uneasily—a foreman whose ancestors homesteaded the ranch and a cook who'd spent at least two-thirds of her life here. There was some serious entrenchment at the True Love. He'd be wise to keep his plans for the property to himself for the time being.

"Dexter came in with the mail a few minutes ago," Belinda said. "I put it in your office."

"Thanks, Belinda."

"Duane and I passed him on the road," T.R. told her. "That seems like quite a hike for a man who has to use a walker."

Freddy's back stiffened. "Dexter Grimes was the best team roper and the finest ranch foreman in southern Arizona until his stroke ten years ago. I think your husband can manage a little walk to the mailbox, don't you, Belinda?"

"I think that walk is what's keeping him alive," Belinda said.

T.R. groaned inwardly. The news just got worse and worse. There was no doubt that Belinda and Dexter Grimes were like a second set of parents to Freddy.

"I'll get you that lemonade," Belinda said. "Anything to eat?"

Freddy glanced questioningly at him.

"No, thanks," he said.

"Maybe some sandwiches for the trail, Belinda," Freddy said. "As soon as Curtis shows up with a change of clothes for Mr. McGuinnes, I'm taking him out for a ride around the ranch."

Belinda paused. "*All* around the ranch?"

"I want to make certain he knows what he's thinking of buying," Freddy explained. "Don't you think that's a good idea?"

Belinda looked over at T.R., and he had the feeling she was trying not to laugh. Maybe she couldn't imagine that a city slicker like him could ride a horse. "I think that's a wonderful idea," she said, and hurried toward the back of the house just as the front door opened.

Curtis, a lanky blond cowboy of about twenty-eight or nine, stepped inside holding a pile of clothes. Duane followed, carrying T.R.'s suitcase, brass-edged briefcase and sport coat over one arm. He had on another pair of boots, equally as scruffy as the ones he'd loaned T.R.

Duane turned to Freddy. "Where're you puttin' him?"

"In the John Wayne Room," Freddy said.

Duane ambled off down a hallway to the right.

T.R. started after him. "I can—"

"Never mind," Freddy said. "Duane will set you up down there. He knows to check around for scorpions and black widows. You might not know where to look."

T.R. controlled a shudder. "You have much problem with that?"

"Not much," Curtis said. "Except for this time of year. The black widows mate about now and lay their eggs. Once they get what they want from the male spider, they kill him, so if you see a web with this petrified shell of a spider in it, that's the luckless husband, and his widow's around somewhere."

T.R. could do without the explanation, coming as it did on the heels of watching a castration.

But Curtis seemed determined to give a lecture in natural history. "And the scorpions, see, they come out at night. The big ones aren't too bad, but those little ones pack quite a—"

"Now, Curtis," Freddy said, laying a hand on his arm. "Mr. McGuinnes won't be sleeping a wink if you carry on like that."

"Please call me T.R.," he said. He'd had enough of this Mr. McGuinnes stuff.

"Initials seems kind of silly," Curtis said. "What do they stand for?"

"Thomas Rycroft."

"Ain't nobody ever called you Tom?"

The comment hit him like a sucker punch to the gut, but years of practice at hiding pain kept his expression neutral. Only one person had ever used that name, and he wasn't about to let anyone sully that memory. "T.R. is fine," he said. "Are these the clothes you brought me, Curtis?"

"Yep." Curtis held them out proudly. "Brought you my newest jeans and a shirt my brother sent me from Abilene. There's a belt there, and the jacket ain't got no rips or anything, either, and I washed it last week."

"Thanks, but I can't imagine I'll need a jacket."

"Oh, yes, you will," Freddy said. "It gets chilly up in Rogue Canyon. Better take it. And Curtis, would you look in that back closet for a hat? I think one of the guests left a black one that should fit."

Duane reappeared from the hallway. "All set in the John Wayne Room."

Curtis returned with a black hat in one hand and glanced at Duane. "You checked real good for black widows and scorpions, didn't ya, Duane?"

Duane looked blank. Then he grinned at Curtis. "Uh, shore I did. Shore. Only killed two, but of course, this is daytime. They come out more at night, you know."

T.R. vowed he'd inspect the room completely before he turned in tonight. Nobody had said anything about tarantulas, but he seemed to remember they lived in Arizona, too. Funny, but bugs had never shown up on the Ponderosa. He accepted the clothes and started toward the hall. Then he turned. "Did John Wayne really sleep there, or is the name just something to impress the tourists?"

"He really slept there," Freddy said. "He made several movies out at Old Tucson. This was one of his favorite places to stay, and that was his special room."

At last, a piece of good news, T.R. thought as he carried his clothes down the hall. That settled it. The developers should definitely leave the ranch house standing and make use of the John Wayne Room somehow. There also had to be a way to get rid of the damned bugs.

CURTIS TURNED to Freddy after T.R. had left the room. "You know, I'm almost beginning to feel sorry for that tenderfoot. The John Wayne stuff is the only true thing he's heard since he got here."

"That's not so, Curtis," Freddy countered. "Everything we've said is true. The ranch is best seen from the back of a horse. We do sometimes have scorpions or black widows around, although the spraying service works pretty well. And you're one to talk about taking pity on him. You gave him new jeans for the trail ride."

Curtis grinned. "I saw right away what you're tryin' to do. Pretty smart. So if he has a bad time out on the trail, he'll go home, right? And then Mr. Whitlock can buy the ranch."

"That's the idea."

Duane adjusted his hat and chuckled. "You shoulda seen his face when you cut Red Devil. But I have to hand it to him, he stuck it out and didn't faint or nothin'."

"He's not a bad guy," Freddy said. "But he's an Easterner, and I can tell he's used to running things and wouldn't leave us alone like Westridge has done. He asked me right away why we didn't cut down the mesquite bosques and sell the wood to fancy restaurants back East. If he buys the ranch, he'll have the power to do just that."

Duane's jaw tightened. "Then you'd better take him on a nice long ride, boss. I may cuss those trees when we have to go in there after our critters, but I wouldn't want that wood to be flavoring somebody's beefsteak in New York City."

"Exactly."

"And I can't picture riding for a boss who calls himself T.R."

"It is stuffy." Freddy had noticed that T.R.'s expression had closed down when Curtis had suggested calling him Tom. She wondered if she'd ever learn what caused the sudden reaction. Probably not. By tomorrow, T. R. McGuinnes would be heaving his saddle-sore body back onto a plane bound for New York, and Eb Whitlock would have a clear shot at the True Love.

"Lemonade," chirped Belinda, sweeping in from the other direction carrying a frosty pitcher and glasses. "I heard you boys out here and went back for more glasses."

"Thanks, Belinda," Freddy said. "You didn't have to serve us yourself."

"Nonsense. Feels good once in a while." She held the tray of drinks toward Freddy. "Besides, I wanted to thank you for trying to keep that Easterner from buying the place. I think you've hit on a wonderful idea."

Freddy took a glass from the tray. "I hope so."

"You know," Belinda said, "I could probably adjust, but really if Dexter and I had to leave . . ."

"I'd do just about anything to keep that from happening, Belinda," Freddy told her.

"I know." Belinda's usually kind expression became flinty. "So would I." She looked over Freddy's shoulder. "And here comes our pigeon now."

Belinda's description made Freddy smile. But when she turned toward the hall, her smile faded. A New York businessman had left the room. Someone with an entirely different aura had returned.

The pearl-buttoned Western shirt, black with a bold gray arrow design across the chest, molded a torso that appeared more muscular than she'd at first suspected. The jeans were snug, too, and looked mighty fine in the front. She didn't need him to turn around to picture how they looked in the back. The black hat was pulled low over his blue eyes, eyes that flashed with a cool kind of fire, as if the clothes had awakened something elemental in him. Sure as shootin', T. R. McGuinnes had turned into cowgirl bait. And she was the one who'd suggested they spend the night together. Her plan had just become more complicated.

3

T.R. LOVED THE FIRST two hours of the trail ride. Despite the heat that baked his back and thighs, he enjoyed the rhythm of the horse beneath him, the acrid scent of sun-warmed bushes and blossom-studded cactus plants, the call of birds and the caress of an occasional cool breeze. The hat shaded his face and the leather saddle cupped his groin in a pleasant grip.

Freddy had assigned him to Mikey, a brown horse with a black mane and tail. Mikey's head bobbed pleasantly as they clopped along the trail behind Freddy's mount, a reddish mare named Maureen, after Maureen O'Hara, one of John Wayne's leading ladies. T.R. had never ridden horseback behind a woman before and hadn't realized how sexy the view could be.

He felt vaguely guilty about his thoughts, but not guilty enough to censor them. Freddy's firm buttocks rested lightly in the saddle as they walked, but brief periods of trotting sent her into a graceful posting motion that was decidedly erotic. His manhood tightened in response to the suggestive movement, but he didn't plan to indulge in anything beyond innocent fantasy. The True Love already had too much emotional baggage for his taste. He wasn't about to add another entanglement by becoming sexually involved with the foreman.

Freddy led him to the south boundary of the ranch, and from there they rode west, then north toward Whitlock's property. T.R. glimpsed clusters of cattle, but they were never close enough to get a really good look. The sales brochure had mentioned a herd of about two hundred female Herefords, ten bulls and whatever calves had been born that spring. Freddy pointed out a twenty-acre horse pasture fenced with barbed wire to separate the horses turned loose in the pasture from the cattle that roamed the rest of the property. Farther on was another fenced pasture that held a scattered herd of approximately a hundred red-and-white Herefords.

"Those belong to Duane," Freddy said over her shoulder. "They carry his brand, the D-Bar. He's working on an experimental breeding project, so we keep his stock separated from ours and lease him the land. Ours forage on whatever they can find, but Duane has to feed this bunch."

"Have you had a roundup yet?" he called ahead to her.

She turned in her saddle. "Three weeks ago. That's the one time we're booked solid because we let the guests help."

T.R. nodded. He was sorry he'd missed that.

As they headed east, toward the mountains, T.R. began to feel discomfort. He checked his watch and realized he'd expected to be back at the ranch by now. Maybe he'd underestimated his endurance.

A short time later, Freddy gestured to her left. "That adobe building over there is the original homestead built by Thaddeus Singleton."

T.R. stood in his stirrups, glad for a reason to stretch and get his behind out of the saddle. He studied the squat, flat-roofed structure that wasn't much bigger than a single-car garage. A hundred years of sun and rain had battered and bleached the earthen blocks; strong winds and animals had knocked holes in the walls. Yet the pioneer in T.R. admired the spirit of the man who had carved out this foothold in a hostile land.

"I can take you a little closer, if you're interested," Freddy said.

He probably shouldn't agree to detours, considering the condition of his thighs, but he didn't want to seem like a wuss, either. "Sure."

As they drew closer, he noticed that a wooden lintel remained in place over the front door, and the ever-present heart with an arrow through it had been burned deep into the wood. In a far corner of the roofless building, the adobe was blackened, as if by fire. "What caused that?" he asked, pointing.

"Hikers staying here for the night, most likely." Freddy leaned her forearms on her saddle horn and gazed at the ruins. "I've found all sorts of evidence of people camping here. Leigh and I have talked about fencing the building off and eventually restoring it, but the corporation hasn't been interested and Leigh and I don't have the money. My grandfather poured that concrete floor in the thirties, back when the roof was still intact and we used this place for temporary shelter if we were caught out here in bad weather. That's the last improvement the place had."

"I see." He wasn't interested in preservation. Attach too much sentimentality to the place by creating a shrine to the original homesteader, and future developers might run afoul of the historic preservation police. He wanted this prize parcel to be unencumbered when it went on the block.

"Thaddeus's wife, Clara Singleton, once held off a raiding party of twenty Apaches from the roof of that house," Freddy said. "The parapet was about three feet high back then, and she used a ladder to climb up and pulled it after her. She had three guns there, and she crawled around firing them in succession, so the Apaches thought there were more people at the house. Thaddeus was off rounding up strays. She drove off those Apaches all by herself."

"That's quite a story." T.R. had noticed the defiant tilt of her chin, the flash in her eyes as she told it. No one could doubt that Freddy had inherited courage and determination from Clara Singleton. Unfortunately, in this modern-day struggle for control of the True Love, he and his partners would be cast in the role of marauding Apaches, and this time the Singleton women were outgunned.

"Clara was quite a woman." Freddy clicked her tongue and urged Maureen down the trail with a nudge of her heels. "There's a dry wash up ahead," she called over her shoulder. "Want to lope the horses a little?"

"Sure." Maybe a good run would release some of the tension building in him. He'd thought that after fifteen years of commodities trading, he'd be immune to attacks of conscience about making money from the misfortunes of others. The free-enterprise system produced the healthiest economy in the world, but you had to play by the rules. People made money or went broke according to the demands of the market, and woe to the investor who worried about the hindmost.

He eased Mikey down a rocky embankment into a wide sandy riverbed littered with tree branches rubbed smooth by rushing water. He'd heard about flash floods and imagined this was the sort of place one would happen. But the sky was an unrelenting blue.

With a whoop and a flick of her reins against Maureen's polished rump, Freddy took off down the wash. With no prompting, Mikey leaped after her, and T.R grabbed the saddle horn with one hand and his hat with the other.

After the first moment of surprise, he gripped the horse with his thighs, crammed the hat more firmly on his head, and grasped the reins as he leaned into the wind. A fantasy created by years of Saturday-afternoon matinees came true in that moment—T. R. McGuinnes, famous gunslinger, galloped his cow pony under an endless sky, the hot wind flattening his Western shirt against his chest and whipping the horse's mane against the backs of his hands. As he drew alongside Freddy, he looked over at her. She grinned at him, and in that pell-mell moment, with his heart pumping from the excitement of the run, he experienced a rush of emotion that scared the hell out of him. Immediately, he began reining in his horse. Within five seconds, T. R. McGuinnes, commodities trader and emotional conservative, was back in the saddle.

FREDDY NOTICED signs of strain in T.R. by the time they reached the pond that served as a reservoir for the True Love. An earthen dam cradled the waters of Rogue Creek about a third of the way up Rogue Canyon, and it was one of Freddy's favorite spots on the ranch.

T.R. winced as he dismounted and looked longingly at the cool water, as if he'd like nothing better than to strip and immerse himself in it. But to his credit, he didn't complain. Freddy began to wonder what it would take to wring a protest out of him.

Choosing her favorite flat rock under the shade of a large cottonwood, she tethered Maureen to a low branch and dug in her saddlebag for the sandwiches Belinda had given her. She'd also brought along some dehydrated stew that she'd brew up for their dinner, and each saddle had a bedroll tied to the cantle, but she didn't want to announce their overnight plans yet. She wanted to be far enough into the canyon that T.R. wouldn't consider finding his own way back to a Jacuzzi and a soft bed. She sat down and watched him, wondering how he'd take the news.

T.R. tied Mikey's reins to the same branch Freddy had used for Maureen and gingerly lowered himself to the rock. He'd obviously forgotten to bring his canteen when he'd dismounted, so she offered hers.

"Oh!" He started to get up. "I have a—"

"Never mind." She pulled on his arm to bring him back beside her. "We can share."

"You first," he said.

She took a sip, wiped the rim on her sleeve, and offered it to him. Funny, she'd shared a canteen with riding partners all her life, yet she'd never been so aware of the intimacy of the act. Maybe it was the way he'd glanced at her mouth before he accepted the container of water.

He started to drink, and paused. "Can we refill our canteens from the pond?"

"Yes." She was impressed that he'd thought to ask. Some tenderfeet would have gulped the contents of the canteen and worried about their water supply after it was exhausted. "Besides, I have a couple more jugs in my saddlebag."

"Good." He tipped his head back and swallowed continuously until the canteen was empty. Like a schoolgirl, she watched him, noticing the surprising length of his eyelashes as he closed his eyes and the generous curve of his lower lip as it cupped the mouth of the canteen. A drop of moisture escaped and trickled down his chin. She had the sudden urge to lean over and lick it off. Good thing she'd planned this so he'd most likely be on a plane to New York by tomorrow, or no telling what stupid thing she might do. Her commitment to the ranch allowed no time for romance. Leigh had accused her of throwing herself into ranch work in order to compensate for not having a man in her life, but what did Leigh know?

By the time T.R. had finished drinking, Freddy was busy unwrapping a sandwich. She handed it to him with brisk efficiency and began eating her own.

"Where did the name of the ranch come from?" he asked. "The real estate broker didn't seem to know."

Freddy was offended. In her opinion, no one should be allowed to market her ranch without understanding its history. "When Thaddeus announced he was marrying Clara, the churchgoing people around here had a fit," she began. "Clara was a dance-hall girl, and some said she sold her favors."

"Sold her favors." T.R. smiled. "Such a quaint way of putting it. Do you think she did?"

Freddy looked into his blue eyes and a curl of awareness snaked through her midsection. They were, after all, talking about sex. "Probably. Back then, a single girl could either teach school, take in laundry or entertain men for a living. Clara didn't have any education, and from what I know of her, she wasn't the type to wash other people's dirty shirts."

"Sounds like a feisty woman." There was a note of approval in his voice.

"She was. And Thaddeus was determined to have her, regardless of the wagging tongues. When they were married, he named the ranch the True Love to show those busybodies he didn't give a hoot about their opinion."

"Good for him."

Freddy crumpled her sandwich wrapping. "He was true to her, and she to him, until the day she died, forty-three years later."

"I'll bet he was true to her even after that."

She looked into his eyes and her heart stumbled. Not many men would chance making such a sentimental remark. "He probably was," she said, a bit hypnotized by the depth of emotion in his gaze. She gave herself a mental shake. "If you'll fill the canteens, we can head up the canyon," she said, starting to rise.

"Sure." His slight groan as he pushed himself to his feet elicited sympathy from her instead of the satisfaction she'd hoped to feel. He walked stiffly to his horse, retrieved his canteen and returned slowly to the water's edge with their two containers. He crouched, dipped the canteens in the water and clenched his jaw as he stood. "This is a nice spot," he said, his tone conversational as he glanced at the granite walls rising on either side of them. She could imagine what it cost him to make pleasant comments when his thigh and groin muscles were very likely screaming in protest. "How long has it been here?"

"Thirty years. My dad decided to dam up Rogue Creek and create a pond. He got sick of going to the mountains to fish, so he stocked it with bass."

"Why is it called Rogue Creek?"

"Because it's in Rogue Canyon."

He rolled his eyes.

"The truth is, my great-grandfather had to come up here after a rogue cougar. He shot the cougar, but not before the cougar almost killed his horse."

T.R. looked uneasy. "Are there any still living up here?"

"A few." Her conscience prickled her. "But you'll probably never see one. They usually keep away from people."

"Fine with me." He glanced back at the pond. "What if the ranch wanted to tap into this pond?"

"Why would we?"

"Say you wanted to put in more landscape plants, maybe a greater area in grass."

Freddy gave herself a mental slap for softening toward this dude. He was an Easterner, and the first thing most Easterners wanted to do was green up the desert and make it look like the Boston Common. For all she knew, the guy had plans to build the True Love Golf Course out behind the corrals. "We try to keep our watering needs low by using plants that don't require much moisture," she said. "Ready to go? I want to show you the Forest Service land where we summer the cattle."

"Lead on." Only the faintest flicker of his eyelashes betrayed his pain as he settled himself in the saddle once more.

BY FIVE O'CLOCK, T.R. wondered if he'd ever walk normally again. By six, he wondered if he'd ever walk again, period. And his feet weren't the problem. He wasn't a tenderfoot, he was a tenderass. He envisioned Duane and Curtis lifting him from Mikey's broad back with his legs frozen in a permanent bow. He'd have to order a custom-made chair for his office in New York, one with inches of padding and a spacious enough seat to accommodate the new wide-open configuration of his thighs.

They'd climbed for most of the afternoon. Cactus and sage had given way to something he recognized as belonging to the oak family and a type of evergreen with a fragrant bark, probably some sort of cedar. He supposed it was beautiful, if he could only give a damn. Who would have imagined that riding around the ranch could take this long? Surely they'd have to turn back soon, although he didn't relish the idea of riding downhill and trying to keep his aching private parts from sliding forward against the saddle horn.

He could hardly believe he'd begun this ride having sensual thoughts about the woman in front of him. He couldn't imagine ever using his bruised equipment again. She'd not only crippled him, she'd ruined his future sex life. The crisp jeans that had made him feel like such a stud this morning now felt like chain mail wrapped around his genitals in an imitation of a medieval chastity belt.

One image kept him going; one reward beckoned at the end of this torture trail. He pictured the Jacuzzi he'd seen beside the swimming pool, pictured himself being carried to it, eased into the water and left there for days. The image almost made him weep with longing.

He was so engrossed in his suffering that he didn't notice Freddy had stopped on the trail and he nearly ran Mikey up Maureen's backside. Mikey realized the problem, snorted and backed up a step.

Freddy swiveled in her saddle and smiled at him. "How are you doing?"

Dammit, he wouldn't give her the satisfaction of knowing the truth. "Fine," he said.

"Time has gone by so quickly this afternoon." She gazed out across the mountain slope. "I doubt if we could make it back before dark, so I thought we'd just camp over there, against that cliff."

He tried to clear the haze of pain from his mind. He could have sworn she'd said they were about to camp.

No Jacuzzi. No bed. Sleeping on the ground. How could he do that if he couldn't even get off his horse by himself? Would she notice if he quietly stayed on his horse and slept in the saddle?

"T.R.?"

He focused on her with effort. "What?"

"Are you okay?" She looked concerned.

He felt his machismo slipping. "Depends on your definition."

"It has been a rather long ride, at that."

"Really? I hadn't noticed."

"Follow me," she said, a gentle note in her voice.

Mikey followed. T.R. had lost the ability to guide Mikey several hours ago.

"Stay there," she said as she swung down and tied Maureen's reins to an oak tree. "I'll help."

Pride asserted itself. "I'm fine," he insisted, and in one brave movement hoisted his leg over Mikey's rump. Somebody yelled, and as he stumbled to the ground, he recognized his own cry of pain. Freddy caught him before he went all the way down and lowered him to a seat on a fallen tree.

"Sit here," she said. "I'll set up camp."

As if he had any choice. He sat and glared at Mikey, instrument of his undoing. His thigh muscles throbbed, and the family jewels felt as if Mikey had kicked him dead center. "Some friend you are," he grumbled at the horse. Mikey yawned, exposing big yellow teeth. "You might have warned me that an all-day ride would turn me into a eunuch."

"Maybe this will help," Freddy said.

He gazed up, bleary-eyed, at the opened flask she extended. "What is it, hemlock?"

"Whiskey. I always carry some in my saddlebag. You never know when it'll come in handy."

"Oh, yeah, for when you have to dig out a bullet after a battle with the rustlers, right?" he said sarcastically.

She pulled the flask away. "If you're going to be like that—"

"No, please. I'd like some." He accepted the flask and took a swig in what he hoped was a manly fashion. The whiskey was strong, at least eighty proof, and he welcomed its punch. He started to hand the flask back to her but she waved it away.

"Keep it. I'll fix us some dinner."

"I suppose you have to go out and shoot it first, this being the Wild West and all."

She stood eyeing him, her hands on her hips. "You do have a wisecracking streak in you, McGuinnes."

"It's either that or hysteria. I thought I'd wisecrack for a while."

A smile tugged at the corners of her mouth. "You told me you could ride."

He straightened as best he could. "I can," he said with as much dignity as he could muster. "For brief periods."

She covered her mouth, where he suspected a smile had broken through. Then she coughed into her fist. "Have a few more pulls on that flask, and when you feel ready, take off your pants."

"Excuse me?"

"So you can massage some Bag Balm into your thighs," she said, barely swallowing a chuckle.

"*Bag Balm?*"

"Aren't you feeling a bit—uh—chafed?"

"What if I am?"

"This is a lanolin-based product. We use it on the cows' udders to keep them soft and—"

"My God."

Tears of laughter brimmed in her eyes. "Believe me, it will help. And some liniment for your feet and knees will keep you from being so stiff in the morning."

His eyes narrowed as a suspicion worked its way through his pain-clouded brain. "How come you're so well equipped for this emergency?"

"Well—"

"You knew this would happen, didn't you?"

"I suspected it might."

"Is this some sort of greenhorn ritual?"

Her smile faded. "Not exactly. This land tests people, and that's something you should know up front."

"You test people, too, don't you?"

"Maybe I do. But I meant what I said about appreciating the True Love with a ride like this. If you can manage to turn around, you might understand what I was talking about. The only way to really see it is by coming up here on horseback."

The whiskey had dulled the sharp edge of his agony, and with effort he eased his legs over the trunk so he was facing the opposite direction.

The view stole his breath. The valley spread beneath them, honey gold in the setting sun. He picked out the U-shaped roofline of the ranch house with the pool inset like a chip of turquoise. Some distance away, the corrals resembled a tic-tac-toe design against the dun color of the bladed earth. Nearer, a flash of light indicated where the pond lay, its surface gilded by lingering sunbeams.

Land. His land, and his partners' land, if he wanted it enough. He'd never owned even a square foot of anything. He'd lived in leased apartments all his adult life and had never minded the lack of ownership. Until now.

Surveying the wide sweep of the True Love's holdings, a new hunger filled him.

"Where's the eastern boundary?" he asked, keeping his gaze fixed on the panorama.

"We crossed it about a mile above the pond. We're standing on Forest Service land, of which we lease a thousand acres."

"That much?"

"We need it to run the herd we have."

"Do you bring Duane's cattle up here, too?"

Freddy chuckled and shook her head. "He'd never let those precious critters run around loose up here. They might lose an ounce or chip a hoof."

A hundred and sixty acres, T.R. thought. And a thousand more leased for grazing. It seemed an immense chunk to a guy who lived in nine-hundred-square feet of space in Manhattan. "It's a lot of land," he murmured.

"Yes, although not compared to seventy years ago. Thaddeus and Clara were able to homestead twice as much, three hundred and twenty acres. But in the time since they died, pieces had to be sold off to take care of debts. Eb Whitlock bought a hundred acres twenty-five years ago."

"To think the ranch was twice this big once. I wish I could have seen it in the glory days of cattle ranching."

Freddy sighed. "I wish I could have, too."

They stood in silence as the crimson sun eased below a horizon trimmed with a rickrack of mountains. T.R. wondered if he'd ever watched the sun set before in all his thirty-five years. He'd had no idea what he'd been missing.

4

FOR AN EASTERNER, T.R. was handling himself pretty well, Freddy thought as she collected wood for a fire. She'd expected him to be in a nasty mood by now, but the whiskey and the sunset over the valley had mellowed him considerably. She'd left him on the log with the flask of whiskey while she completed the routine chores of setting up camp. In short order she'd unsaddled the horses, draped the pads over the saddles to dry and hobbled Mikey and Maureen in a nearby clearing where they could graze.

The altitude and lack of sun was cooling the dry air quickly. Greenhorns like T.R. didn't realize a drop of nearly forty degrees was common in the desert at night. He'd need that jacket he'd been reluctant to bring, and the warmth of a fire, as well. And the Bag Balm and liniment. Considering the lack of privacy the camp provided, she wondered if T.R. would have the nerve to take off his clothes and apply the remedies.

As she crouched next to the fire and stirred the packet of dried stew into a small pot of water, the sound of shuffling footsteps announced his arrival behind her.

"Smells pretty good," said a voice tight with pain.

She glanced over her shoulder. He stood a few feet away, his legs braced and his expression grim beneath the shadow of his hat. He'd finished about half the flask, which probably explained how he'd managed to walk at all. Her heart swelled with remorse. Dammit, she should have known she was too softhearted to pull this off, especially when her target was taking his punishment with such good grace.

"If you'll tell me where the medication is, I'll get it."

"No, let me." She laid the spoon on a piece of aluminum foil, stood and walked over to the pile of gear. After rummaging through the saddlebag, she found the tin of Bag Balm and the liniment bottle. "Here," she said, walking toward him. "It won't work miracles, but it might make the ride out tomorrow more bearable."

He flinched at the reminder that he'd be remounting Mikey in the morning. "Thanks." Keeping the flask in one hand, he cradled the tin and bottle in his other arm while he hobbled back toward the fallen tree.

She watched him go and knew he'd never be able to manage the therapy alone. What had she been thinking? "T.R.," she called, going after him. "Maybe I should ride for help. We could bring a helicopter in here, maybe even tonight if I hurry."

He turned, his expression incredulous. "A helicopter? You've got to be kidding."

"Look, you've proved you can take a beating, so why—"

"Not on your life." Teeth clenched, he eased back to the log and set the flask, the liniment and the Bag Balm on the ground next to him. "Would any self-respecting cowboy call Search and Rescue?" He took off his hat and mopped his damp forehead with his shirtsleeve.

"You're not a cowboy. You're a commodities trader from New York."

He glanced up. "Even commodities traders have their pride, Freddy," he said quietly. "Don't take that away from me."

"But you didn't know what you were getting into! You don't have to tough it out like some stereotypical cowboy. This is my fault, not yours!"

A smile flickered across his face. "I was wondering when you'd admit you deliberately ambushed me."

She averted her eyes. "I wanted to discourage you from buying the ranch."

"Why? Somebody will, sooner or later, and you don't own it now, anyway."

She mustered her composure and faced him. "Eb Whitlock wants it, but he doesn't have the kind of money you do. Eb's a neighbor and a friend. He'll let me keep running the ranch."

"And you thought I'd fire you? After you've proved how valuable you are to the whole operation?"

"You're an Easterner. Who knows what you would do?"

"Never trust anybody who comes from east of the Mississippi, is that it?"

She lifted her chin. "Works for me."

With a sigh, he settled his hat on the log beside him.

"But I'm . . . sorry I've crippled you," she added. "You didn't really deserve that."

"What if this experience sours me on the True Love and I decide against buying it, just like you planned? Will you be sorry then?"

She looked into his blue eyes, sharp with pain. "Yes, I'll still be sorry. It was a dirty trick and I apologize. Why don't you let me ride down and arrange for a helicopter?"

"No." He took a swig from the flask and contemplated his boots.

"I don't think you can get those off by yourself."

"Of course I can." He leaned slowly forward. "I—
augh!" He straightened and passed a hand over his face.
"And to think only this morning I could tie my own
shoes."

"Here." Freddy straddled his leg, her backside to him,
and took hold of his boot heel. "Resist me on the count
of three."

"In this condition, I'll be able to resist you no matter
how long you count."

"Very funny. Now get ready. One, two, *three!*" She
yanked and he yelled, but the boot came off. "Now the
other one." She repeated the procedure, then turned to
face him, looking directly into his eyes. "Now the pants."

Defiance flashed in the blue depths. "I can—"

"It'll be faster and easier if I help you." A heavy load
of guilt pushed her to press on in this mission of mercy.
"This is no time to be modest, T.R. You need that Bag
Balm applied as soon as possible. Imagine yourself as a
patient in the emergency room of a hospital."

"I usually try to avoid the hospital if I can help it."

"And no woman has even taken off your pants?"

He took another drink from the flask and impaled her
with a look. "I didn't say that."

To her dismay, she flushed, which completely destroyed the air of sophistication she'd been striving to
maintain, but she barreled on, just the same. "Take off
your belt and unbutton your jeans. I'll work them off
from the ankles."

He held her gaze while he complied, and she met his
challenge for as long as she could before looking away.
She suspected the liquor he'd imbibed accounted for the
bold stare. The trail ride had been a dumb idea, she decided. She'd thought that by tomorrow she'd be cele-

brating her victory over the briefcase-carrying businessman who had tried to steal her ranch. Except that T.R. was no longer an impersonal enemy, but a vulnerable man in pain. A sexy man in pain. And that was the crux of the problem.

"I'm ready." He was still regarding her with the same intensity. Only now his jeans were unfastened and his hands were braced on either side of him in what had to be an unconscious gesture of invitation, considering his condition. "Got a bullet for me to bite down on?"

"You've seen too many movies." Taking a deep breath, she squatted between his ankles. As she tugged on the stiff denim, breath hissed between his teeth. She paused.

"Just keep going."

Trying to remain focused on his ankles, she worked the material down. His socks came with the jeans, and finally she was forced to grasp the waistband and pull it past his calves. The job couldn't be done without touching him, but she tried to minimize contact. In spite of her efforts, her fingers encountered firm muscle and the tantalizing brush of hair. She swallowed and wrenched the jeans over his feet with more force than was necessary. He gasped, but didn't cry out.

"There." With a sigh of relief, she got to her feet. Her relief was short-lived. One glimpse and she realized that a half-clothed T. R. McGuinnes, even put out of commission by an all-day ride, was a sight to triple the heart rate of any normal female. From the looks of his powerful legs, he was well acquainted with the inside of a gym. With a new pang of conscience, she realized he'd make a good rider someday, if she hadn't just ruined the experience for him.

He took a glob of Bag Balm from the tin and began dabbing it over the inside of his thighs.

"Not like that," she said before she could stop herself.

He glanced up, a devilish look in his eyes, a crooked smile on his mouth. "You want to show me how?" he said softly.

Now she'd really done it.

"Think of this as a hospital emergency room," he added, holding out the tin of cream.

She'd come this far in her rescue, and if he didn't apply the Bag Balm correctly, it wouldn't do much good. With grave misgivings, she accepted the tin. Kneeling beside him, she smoothed the ointment over the inside of his chafed thigh, applying enough pressure to work it into his skin.

He groaned.

"I have to massage it in a little or it won't penetrate," she apologized. "I know the muscles underneath are sore, too."

"If this didn't hurt so much," he said with obvious effort, "I think it would be lots of fun."

Freddy wasn't about to comment. Instead, she concentrated on covering the reddened area with the ointment. Not far from her circling fingertips, his briefs enclosed an impressive bulge of manhood. She tried to ignore it as she spread ointment on his other thigh. As she settled into her massaging motion, he groaned again. She recognized it as the sound of pain, not ecstasy, but her capricious imagination transformed the low, husky protest into a moan of desire. The image of T.R. making love to her sent tendrils of heat curling through her body.

She looked up into his face. His eyes were closed, his head thrown back, his jaw rigid in response to the pain. But the expression wasn't unlike that of a man in the throes of orgasm. Her pulse quickened. She remembered the effect he'd had on her when he'd stepped into the living room of the ranch house dressed in jeans, shirt, boots and hat. There had been an air of command about him then. She'd robbed him of that in the past few hours, but if it ever reasserted itself, T. R. McGuinnes would be a man to reckon with.

His hand covered hers, stopping her movement. "That's enough," he said, his voice rough.

She glanced up to find his gaze conveying an unmistakable sexual message. She pulled her hand away and sat back on her heels, her heart pounding.

His smile was wry. "It seems I can't resist you, after all. Maybe you'd better tend the stew while I get myself under control."

One swift look confirmed that he had become aroused during the treatment. She blushed. "I'm sorry. I didn't think—"

"Believe me, neither did I."

"The—the liniment should be put on your knees and feet."

"I'll do it in a minute."

"Then I'll get dinner ready." She jumped to her feet and headed over toward the fire, which seemed cool in contrast to T.R.'s warm gaze. Damn! Her plan to make a fool of this Easterner was in shambles, and in the long run, the fool had turned out to be her.

Two hours later, they'd managed to smooth over the awkwardness between them by ignoring the incident altogether. They sat by the fire drinking coffee laced with the last of the whiskey.

T.R. leaned against the face of the cliff, a bedroll under him and his jacket covering his bare legs. "I suppose I can expect all sorts of poisonous bugs to show up in my bedroll tonight," he said.

"I think the smell of that horse liniment will keep them away."

"So that's why you're sitting on the other side of the fire."

"You've got that right." Actually, the smell of horse liniment didn't bother her all that much. She'd just decided to keep herself as far from temptation as possible during the long night ahead.

T.R. chuckled. "Bag Balm and horse liniment. The funny thing is, I'm having a pretty good time."

"That's because you've finished off that flask."

"Partly. But partly because we're camping out. I've never done that before."

"Not even in Boy Scouts?"

T.R. shook his head. "I got into sports early—Pop Warner Football League, Little League baseball. I didn't have time for Scouts."

"What positions did you play?"

"Quarterback on the football team, pitcher in base-ball."

Freddy nodded. "The power positions. They proba-bly called you T.R. when you were nine years old."

He sipped his coffee. "Tommy."

"Really?" She decided to be bold and see if she could unravel one of the mysteries about him. "Then I don't understand why you didn't make the natural progres-sion to Tom."

He gazed into the fire for a long moment. "That's what my wife, Linda, said. She refused to call me by a set of initials. Called it stuffy."

A wife. Somehow, Freddy hadn't thought there was a wife. "She's right."

"Was right," he corrected in a monotone. "She's dead."

"Oh!" Understanding hit Freddy like a blow. She remembered how he'd looked when he'd said Thaddeus must have loved Clara even after her death. Apparently, T.R. still loved his wife. "I'm sorry. I didn't know."

"It's okay. I don't talk about it much."

Freddy stared into her coffee mug. Of course he wouldn't want some cowpoke like Curtis calling him by the name his wife had used. But he wasn't the type to broadcast his personal tragedy, either. Under normal circumstances, she doubted he would have told her, a relative stranger, but there was something about a camp fire that encouraged confidences. And he had consumed most of the flask of whiskey.

She waited without much hope to see if he'd add any details. When he didn't, she refrained from asking. "If it were my choice, I'd call you Ry," she said at last.

"Ry?"

"Isn't your middle name Rycroft?"

"I'm surprised you remembered."

So was she. The number of things that stuck in her mind concerning him were beginning to disturb her. "It's an unusual name, that's all."

"So's Freddy. I thought you were a man."

"Would it have made everything easier if I had been?"

He studied her across the dancing flames. "You tell me. Would a man have trailed me over the ranch until I was so saddle-sore I couldn't stand? Would Thaddeus have done that?"

"If his ranch was at stake, he would have. Duane and Curtis thought it was a terrific idea."

"So everybody was in on it?"

"Why do you suppose you got a brand-new pair of jeans guaranteed to make your ride even more miserable?"

He snorted and shook his head. "You people are tough."

"Out here, we have to be."

"Well, let me tell you something. Wall Street is no baby's playground, either."

"I'm sure that's true, but the stakes aren't as high."

His eyebrows lifted. "You don't consider financial ruin a high-stakes game?"

"Not compared to losing the thing you love most."

The transformation in his expression was dramatic. All the challenge and good humor left his eyes, to be replaced by a stark sorrow that seemed to have no bottom. "You're right, of course."

She felt like hell. What a thing to have said to a man whose wife had died. "Sorry again. I seem to be putting my foot in my mouth on a regular basis."

"Never apologize for telling the truth, Freddy." He finished his coffee and stretched gingerly out on the bedroll. "So you think I should change my name."

"You don't seem like the kind of guy who goes by initials."

"What kind is that?"

She hesitated. "A little on the pompous side."

To her relief, he glanced over at her and laughed. "It's not easy being pompous around you. Maybe I've been heading in that direction, though. Is Ry a good name for a cowboy?"

"An excellent name."

"Then maybe I'll try it for a while." He turned his head to look up into the sky. "I had no idea there were so many stars."

"City lights block them out." Pleased that he'd accepted her nickname for him, she threw another stick on the fire and watched the sparks climb into the cool night air. Then she slipped off her boots and lay down on her own bedroll. "But then, I've never seen the lights of Times Square. I guess each place has its own kind of beauty."

He was quiet, and she wondered if he'd fallen asleep. A series of sharp yips drifted up from the valley. "Are those ranch dogs?" he asked.

"Coyotes."

"I thought they were supposed to howl."

"Most Easterners think that. But they yip. Which makes the dogs go crazy. Can you hear them?"

"Yeah. Noise really travels out here."

Her eyelids grew heavy. "Yes."

"I'm glad you brought me up here, even if your motives weren't pure."

"You've been a good sport."

"Thanks. Good night, Freddy." His voice seemed to caress her name, sending unexpected goose bumps over her skin.

"Good night . . ." She hesitated. "Ry."

She awoke to an unidentifiable scream. Bolting from her bedroll, she saw the man she'd recently dubbed Ry crouched against the cliff, a glowing stick he'd plucked from the fire brandished in one hand.

"What is it?" she called.

"I don't know. Get over here."

She was halfway around the fire before she realized she was obeying his command on her territory. The scream came again, followed by the sound of wild snorting and stomping hooves. "It's the horses!" she cried, hurrying back to her bedroll where she pulled on her boots before locating her flashlight and her Smith & Wesson. "Most likely a snake or cougar disturbing them."

"Damn, where are my boots?" he asked.

"Stay put. I'll handle it."

He grunted with pain. "The hell you will."

Ignoring him, she turned on the flashlight and shone it in the direction of the scream. "It's okay, Maureen," she called, setting out through the underbrush. "I'm coming, Mikey. Hang in there." She was counting on the sound of a human voice to discourage whatever critter was after the horses. But if her voice didn't work, her aim with the Smith & Wesson would. She hoped she wouldn't have to use the gun. By coming up this canyon, she knew that she'd invaded the territory of several desert dwellers who had a right to protect themselves, but she had to safeguard her horses.

She found Mikey and Maureen quivering in the clearing where she'd left them, yet a sweep of the flashlight revealed nothing in the area that might have spooked them.

"See anything?" Ry said from behind her.

Freddy sighed in irritation as she continued searching the bushes and overhead branches with the beam of her flashlight. "No, but go back to camp. I don't want to have to worry about you, too."

"No dice."

"Look, you know nothing about the dangers out here. You—where do you think you're going?"

Ry pushed past her and limped over to Mikey. "Shine the light on his hind leg."

She did, and gasped. It was dripping blood. "Oh, my God." She hurried over and crouched beside the horse, whose flanks were heaving. "Easy, Mikey. Easy, boy. Ry, hold his head so I can check this out."

While Ry stroked Mikey's nose and murmured to him, Freddy took a bandanna from her pocket and dabbed at the blood until she could see the wound, a jagged cut just above his fetlock. A little deeper and Mikey would have been crippled for life. As it was, he couldn't be ridden back down the mountain. "I'm going to look Maureen over," she said, moving carefully around the quivering Mikey to her own horse.

The whites of Maureen's eyes showed, and she tossed her head when Freddy reached for her, but after a few moments, the mare settled down. She was unhurt, which meant Ry could ride her down while Freddy led Mikey. "Let's take them back to camp and tether them to a tree," she suggested. "I'll lead Mikey if you'll take Maureen."

"I've got Mikey." Ry coaxed the horse forward and the animal complied with an air of trust that astonished Freddy. Both man and horse limped back to camp.

He just might make a cowboy, at that, Freddy thought. He was stubborn enough. And gutsy. After a few hours of being immobilized in sleep, he must have stiffened up considerably, yet he'd torn himself from his bedroll and snatched a weapon before she was fully awake. She had a gun; he had nothing but a stick, and he'd assumed the role of protector without thinking. Definitely the sort of thing a cowboy would do.

After they secured the horses to an oak tree, she cleaned Mikey's wound with water and applied an antiseptic ointment from her first-aid kit while Ry soothed the horse.

"What do you think happened?" Ry asked after they'd built up the fire and were sitting across from each other on their bedrolls, both too keyed up to sleep.

"I'm not sure. I suppose a snake or a cougar could have spooked them, and Mikey might have ripped his leg open on a jagged rock or broken tree limb lying on the ground."

"Another rogue cougar, maybe?"

Freddy shook her head. "A rogue would have killed at least one of the horses. We'll probably never know what happened."

"Is the injury serious?"

"It could have been. As it is, I'll have to lead him down and you'll have to ride Maureen."

"I'll lead him down."

"Oh, for heaven's sake. You will not."

"Yes, I will. It can't be any worse to walk that trail than to ride it again."

Freddy chuckled. "And here I was beginning to think you were turning into a cowboy."

"What's that supposed to mean?"

"A real cowboy will saddle up to ride from one side of his front yard to the other, rather than walk it."

"That may be true, but if he has to walk so his woman can ride, I'll bet he'd do that."

His woman. She was certain he'd only used the expression to make a point, and it was a chauvinistic thing to say, anyway. So why did she feel a little glow of pleasure? Why did she turn the phrase over in her mind, listening to it again as if it were a refrain from a favorite song? The pressure of the impending sale must be getting to her. Perhaps, deep in her heart, she longed for a white knight to rescue her and give her back the True Love. Maybe she longed for a white knight, period. Being alone all night with an attractive man reminded her of a seldom-acknowledged emptiness in her life. But if she imagined a commodities trader from New York was the answer to her prayers, she must have accidentally dropped a sprig of locoweed into tonight's supper.

5

T.R. DOZED FITFULLY while leaning against the granite face of the cliff. The rock retained heat from the sun that had bathed it during the day, and the warmth soothed his stiff shoulders. An owl hooting in the gray light of dawn brought him awake, and he glanced across the embers of the camp fire to where Freddy lay with her boots still on, her gun within reach. The owl hadn't disturbed her sleep, probably because she was used to the sounds of wildlife in the desert.

Her hair had come free of the clip and lay spread over her outstretched arm; her lips were parted, her expression relaxed and open. He used to love watching Linda sleep, because it was one of the moments when he glimpsed her soft, vulnerable side. The other was when they were making love.

Linda. She would have hated this trail ride, he realized with a smile. Born and bred to big-city life, she'd barely tolerated outdoor cafés, let alone picnics. Freddy, on the other hand, would feel imprisoned in an office, flail her wings against the walls of a hotel room. In that way, the two women were total opposites, and yet Freddy had that same iron will that had drawn him to Linda. And rarer still, the same sense of fair play. She hadn't been able to pull off her diabolical scheme without confessing, without trying to right the wrong she'd done. She could have pushed her plan to the limit, and without the whiskey and horse liniment, he might have checked out of the True Love today and never looked back.

He was still tempted to give up the whole crazy idea. God, he hurt. He'd become used to the smell of the liniment, but even the slightest movement was agony. Walking the entire trail sounded like torture, but the prospect of riding down wasn't much of an improvement. Freddy deserved every pang of conscience that pricked her, he decided.

But whenever he started plotting revenge, he reminded himself that she'd done him a favor without realizing it. Tough though the journey had been, he treasured his first view of the valley, a view he wouldn't have enjoyed without Freddy's scheming. He wouldn't have slept outside and seen the stars spread over the night sky like fairy dust, or been given a new name, a name that seemed to fit as well and give him as much confidence as Duane's boots.

If Freddy hadn't tricked him, he wouldn't have awakened to the hoot of an owl and breathed cool morning air, a mixture of evergreen and charred cedar smoke that stirred him more than the most exotic perfume sold on Fifth Avenue. He wanted a piece of this land, the right to gaze up at a sky so clear it hurt his eyes, to sit by a smoldering camp fire and watch the pink glow of dawn creep over the valley, his valley. And Joe's, of course. Maybe even Lavette's.

They would sell the True Love eventually because it would be stupid not to. But maybe he'd use the money to buy another piece of the West and play the game all over again.

The owl hooted again. Ry looked up through the twisted branches of a cedar and saw the almond glow of a pair of eyes. For a few seconds, he met the owl's unblinking gaze. Then, with a heavy flap of wings, the bird lifted above the treeline and soared out over the valley.

"Are you superstitious?"

Ry glanced across the dying fire and saw Freddy lying on her bedroll watching him. "No."

"Some people think owls are a bad omen."

"Too bad for the owls."

"Have you heard about the curse on the True Love?"

He groaned. "Is this phase two of Get the Greenhorn?"

"I suppose you could say that. But if you're considering buying the place, you should know about all the skeletons in the closet, don't you think?"

"Are you making it up as you go, or is this a genuine, certified curse?"

She propped herself up on one elbow. "Okay, I deserved that. But the story has been told around camp fires since Thaddeus homesteaded the ranch. Do you want to hear it or not?"

"Guess I'd better."

Freddy lay back on her bedroll and gazed up at the pink sky. "The story goes that a small tribe of Indians was massacred on the site where the corrals now stand. A unit of cavalry swept in and killed a village of unarmed women and children when the braves were off hunting. Afterward, when the men of the tribe returned, they put a curse on the land and said no white man would ever profit from it."

"I'm surprised they didn't stage a little massacre of their own."

"They tried, but the cavalry handled them easily. It wasn't one of our finer moments in history."

Ry decided he'd keep that story away from any potential buyers, including his partners. It wasn't a pretty tale, and besides, investors became uneasy when you talked about loss of profit, even if it was connected to something as goofy as a century-old curse. "Seems to me Thaddeus knocked the heck out of that prediction."

"Not really." Freddy laced her hands behind her head, a movement that lifted and defined her breasts.

Ry noticed and chastised himself. Freddy would be his foreman, and he'd known too many businessmen who'd ruined an employer-employee relationship by bringing personal attraction into it. "I thought you said Thaddeus owned three hundred and twenty acres before he died."

"Owned is a relative term. He controlled three hundred and twenty acres, but he was in debt. That's been the story all down the line. In terms of having money left over, making what I would call a profit, nobody's done it yet."

"Not even your father?"

"Especially not my father. After my mother died, he spent more time rodeoing than running the ranch. If it hadn't been for Belinda and Dexter, who knows what would have happened to the place."

Ry heard a familiar note in her voice, the same note of frustration he'd felt when his parents divorced and his world had been torn apart. "When did she die?"

"I was fourteen, Leigh was ten."

"That's rough."

She looked over at him. "Lots of kids have it worse. At least I had a horse of my own and plenty of space to ride. Dexter let me go on the roundups, and I could ride a bronc as well as any of the hands."

"I'll bet you still can."

She grinned. "There's nothing like a good bucking horse to put life into proper perspective." Then her smile faded as she gazed at him. "The True Love is great for making you forget your troubles, but I wouldn't say it's a financial gold mine. That's why Westridge is selling, and all they're after is what they put into it. I could get in trouble for telling you that, but I could get in trouble for this whole stunt, I suppose."

"You're right, you could," he said with a straight face. "You should never have admitted a thing, Miss Singleton. I probably have the power to get you fired."

She didn't flinch. He imagined she wore the same look that gunslingers used in the Old West to face down their opponents. "I reckon you have that power," she said evenly. "And probably the right, too."

"You're a fearless woman, Freddy Singleton."

A corner of her mouth turned up. "Just what I wanted you to think."

Damn, but he liked her. "I won't turn you in. For one thing, it's no secret that the property's price can be negotiated downward. I've studied the profit and loss statements. The resorts built recently in Tucson have hurt business and I know Westridge has a cash-flow problem and is eager to sell. By the way, do they know about this so-called curse?"

"No, not really. They just think the ranch is falling apart from age, which it probably is."

"Do you think it's cursed?"

She shook her head. "I'd planned to tell you I did, to help scare you off, but I think we've just had a run of bad luck."

"If it reduces the asking price, it's good luck for me. All I have to offer is enough to squeeze out Whitlock."

"I see." Her gaze hardened. "Somehow, when you're hobbling around a camp fire without your pants, I forget that you're a shark in the business world."

She was quick. He liked that, too. "I wouldn't be name-calling after the trick you pulled on me yesterday," he said. "Shall we just agree that we're fighters, and we can both be ruthless when it comes to getting what we want?"

She studied him, seeming to take his measure as he was taking hers. "*Ruthless* is a harsh word. How about *determined*?"

"*Determined* works."

The smile she gave him, fresh as the morning, made his heart ratchet in his chest. "It's a beautiful day," she said. "The birds are singing and the sky is clear. What do you say we call a truce?"

He'd never been at war, but she did seem to perceive him as the enemy. "Okay. Truce."

BREAKFAST WAS coffee and biscuits, which Ry wolfed down with an appetite that astounded him. Somehow he pulled on his jeans and boots without help from Freddy. With luck, they wouldn't have any more intimate encounters like the one with the Bag Balm. He suspected there was some powerful chemistry at work if he could get aroused in the midst of all that pain. Once he'd looked down and seen her head practically in his lap and caught a glimpse of her supple fingers at work, the power of suggestion had made him instantly hard as a rock. Since then, he'd had stirrings in that direction, but he'd kept a rein on his imagination.

He gave her as much help as he could breaking up camp. Moving around was painful, but exercise helped work the stiffness out of his legs. They used the last of their water on the fire and smothered any remaining embers in sand. Freddy paid more attention to putting out the fire than any of the other leave-taking chores.

"No hydrants up here," she said. "Lightning starts enough fires without people adding to the danger."

"Have you had many fires?"

"More than I cared to." Freddy pointed up above the cliff face. "See that grassy area? Lightning started a fire a few years ago, wiped out all the trees on that slope. Seen from the ranch at night, it was almost pretty, with the mountain glowing like a Christmas decoration, until you realized that the decoration was destroying acres of trees, and that if the wind changed, the fire could sweep down and take the ranch."

"What can you do if the wind changes?"

Her expression clouded. "Everything possible, of course. A few times, we've hosed the perimeter when a fire came too close for comfort. But in the end, if you can't stop it, you take your animals and get out."

"Is that what happened to the old ranch house?"

"No, that was a kitchen fire, which was bad enough. A runaway brushfire is our worst nightmare."

Ry gazed down into the valley at the cluster of buildings and corrals, which seemed suddenly small and defenseless against the devastation he could imagine overtaking it. Fire protection might be an issue with developers. But then he thought of all the fires in the canyons outside Los Angeles, of the multimillion-dollar homes that had succumbed to the flames; people still clamored to live at the edge of wilderness, despite the danger.

"I guess that's about it," Freddy said, tightening the cinch of Maureen's saddle. "You're sure you don't want to ride down?"

"Mikey and I will walk. We've bonded."

Freddy laughed. "I do believe you have. Why don't you go first so I can follow and keep an eye on his hind leg?"

"Sure." Holding Mikey's bridle, Ry surveyed the camp one last time. He was reluctant to leave because he knew the walk would be uncomfortable, but that wasn't the only reason.

Freddy settled herself in the saddle and gathered her reins. "Listen, I could still ride down leading Mikey and send a helicopter back up for you," she said. "Nobody would think the worse of you for it, Ry."

"Oh, no?" He grinned and shoved his hat to the back of his head as he gazed up at her. "Can you picture Duane and Curtis watching that helicopter coming in without their making a few choice comments about the dude from New York who thought he could ride a horse?"

"They'd never say anything to your face."

"What a comfort that would be."

"So, shall I send a chopper?"

"No, you shall not. I can make it. I was stalling because . . . because to tell the truth, I'm sorry the whole thing is over. I had a great time."

Her laughter bounced against the rocky cliff and echoed out into the valley. "The ride crippled you, you smell like a landfill, the horses kept you up all night and you have to walk several miles down a rocky trail to get back home. If this is what you consider a great time, I suggest you get a life," she said, her hazel eyes dancing.

He smiled at her. "I was thinking the same thing." Then he turned and wrapped the end of the reins around his fist. "Come on, Mikey," he said to the horse as they started out of camp. "Let's show the women what grit is all about."

FOLLOWING BEHIND the battered twosome was its own kind of punishment, Freddy decided. The boots Ry had borrowed were made for riding, for occasional dancing, but not for walking down a mountain path. The smooth soles slipped on loose shale, and the heels tilted him forward, sabotaging his balance even more.

A mile down the trail, she called a halt and offered to trade. He wouldn't do it. She was forced to continue behind him and watch the stain of sweat widen across the back of his shirt. She knew he must be thirsty; she certainly was. But they wouldn't be able to drink until they reached the pond, which would take another hour.

He had every right to hate her. If he complained to Westridge and asked for her resignation as a condition of the sale, she couldn't blame him. But the hell of it was, she knew he didn't hate her and wouldn't get her fired. She'd thrown torture after torture at him, and he had the nerve to announce he'd had a great time. Talk about knowing how to hurt a girl!

Ry had his head down watching the trail for loose stones, and Freddy was concentrating so hard on Ry and Mikey that she didn't hear a horse approaching until the little party rounded a bend and Ry came face-to-face with Eb Whitlock's big palomino. Ry stumbled and nearly went down, but he grabbed a bush and kept himself and Mikey steady. Freddy was grateful he'd reached for a smooth-barked manzanita instead of the prickly pear next to it.

"What do we have here?" Eb boomed, reining in Gold Strike.

Freddy smiled. "Eb! What luck. Do you have water?"

"I reckon you need a sight more than water. Your friend looks like he's been rode hard and put away wet."

"I'm okay." Ry pushed his hat to the back of his head and gazed with apparent interest at the man on the palomino. As usual, Eb was decked out in a belt buckle big as a dinner plate and a bolo tie heavy with turquoise.

Freddy realized introductions were in order, although the grapevine had probably already supplied Eb with the identity of the man in front of him. "Eb Whitlock, I'd like you to meet Ry McGuinnes, from New York City."

"Figured as much." Eb handed over his canteen. "Have a drink on me, McGuinnes. Sorry I can't hail you a cab. You look like you could use one." He laughed at his joke, flashing teeth arranged as perfectly as piano keys.

Ry accepted the canteen with a friendly smile. "No problem. Could you hold on to Mikey for a minute?" He thrust the reins into Eb's hand without waiting for a reply, walked over to Freddy and held out the canteen. "Compliments of the man on the very big horse."

Freddy swallowed a burst of laughter. Eb had always ridden huge geldings. Leigh used to say he'd show up on a Clydesdale one of these days. "Thank you," she said, her voice quivering with humor as she met Ry's gaze and accepted the canteen. She could hardly refuse such a gallant gesture, although she was sure Ry needed water more than she did. After one quick gulp, she passed the canteen to him without bothering to wipe the mouth of the jug.

There was a brief flash of awareness in his eyes, as if he'd noticed her omission, before he lifted the canteen to his lips and drank greedily.

She admired the way the trail had toughened his appearance. His cheeks were stubbled with a day's growth of beard and his face had acquired the healthy bronze color of an outdoorsman.

"What happened to Mikey?" Eb asked, breaking into Freddy's absorption in Ry.

"We're not sure," she replied. "Maybe a broken branch or a sharp section of boulder got him."

"Somebody said they saw a big cat up there not long ago."

"If that's what it was, we didn't see it," Freddy said. "We're just lucky Mikey didn't cut himself up any worse."

"I thought I heard a horse scream up here last night," Eb said. "Then this morning, I remembered Curtis or somebody telling me you'd taken the prospective buyer up here, so I decided to investigate, make sure you were okay."

How typical of him, Freddy thought. "You're a good neighbor, Eb."

Eb touched the brim of his hat in a subtle salute. "I try to be, even if it means baby-sitting my competition."

Ry took the canteen from his lips.

"After all, we've known each other for a long time, Freddy," Eb continued. "Why, I remember—"

"Excuse me, but does anybody else want some more water?" Ry asked. "Freddy? Did you get enough?"

"I'm fine." She was amused and somewhat grateful that Ry had broken into Eb's story. Eb was a conscientious neighbor, but he had a tendency to wax nostalgic a little too often.

"Well, then, let's take care of our wounded patient," Ry said. "I believe this is how they do it in the movies." Taking off his hat, he walked up to Mikey and poured the rest of the water into the upended crown of the hat before offering it to the horse. Mikey tossed his head and rolled his eyes. "Come on, Mikey," Ry coaxed, wiggling the hat to make the water slosh inside. "Didn't you ever watch 'Gunsmoke' in reruns?"

Freddy laughed. Ry had just splashed water into a ninety-dollar hat, but it probably needed some seasoning, anyway. "You have the wrong horse. He's a 'Sein-feld' fan."

"Just my luck." Ry adopted a New York City accent. "Try it, Mikey. You'll like it."

The horse snorted and stuck his nose into the hat to suck the water in noisy swallows while Ry exchanged a grin with Freddy.

Eb glanced around and looked impatient. "Tell you what, McGuinnes. You can climb on behind me and I'll lead Mikey down the trail."

"Oh, I couldn't do that, Whitlock." Ry kept his attention on Mikey. "Thanks, anyway."

"Why not? Gold Strike can carry both of us. Hell, he could probably carry a knight in full armor."

"Probably, but I just wouldn't feel right about it." He clamped the dripping hat on his head and handed Eb the empty canteen. "I'll walk with Mikey, if it's all the same to you."

Freddy bit her lip to hide a smile. She figured Ry was telling the literal truth. He'd no more be able to hoist himself up on Gold Strike and spread his legs over that broad back than fly to the moon on gossamer wings.

"Suit yourself." Eb wheeled his big horse, stirring up a cloud of dust that made Ry choke. "By the way," Eb called over his shoulder as he started down the trail, "how do you like the True Love?"

"Love it," Ry called back.

Eb flashed his large teeth again. "Too bad. Oh well, welcome to the neighborhood."

"Thanks, Eb," Freddy called after him. Then she glanced down at Ry. "There you have a real Western gentleman. He wants the True Love so bad he can taste it, but when he finds out you'll probably buy it out from under him, he greets you as his new neighbor."

Ry wiped the grit from his face with the back of his sleeve. "And you could barely tell he hates my guts. What a guy."

"Hates you? I hardly think so! Just because you're both after the same piece of property doesn't mean he takes that personally."

"Oh, it's not just the True Love he's after." Ry wiggled his eyebrows. "He'd like to slap a brand on you, little filly."

"That's ridiculous." She laughed to cover her flush of embarrassment. Leigh had warned her about the same thing, but Eb was old enough to be her father. She wanted to believe his goodwill was motivated by nothing more than neighborly concern. "He's never even asked me to dinner."

"He doesn't have to. He's your neighbor. And he was hoping to buy your ranch. That would put him in a pretty sweet spot, being your boss and all."

Freddy looked away from his penetrating gaze. "You're making some big assumptions on very little evidence."

"I'm sure it seems that way, but I make my living playing hunches. I make a pretty good living, so I've learned to follow my instincts. Trust me, Whitlock hated me on sight, first because I threaten his acquisition of the ranch, and second because he perceives me as a possible threat to his acquisition of you."

Heat swept over her. "Why would he think that?"

"Easy. I just spent the night alone with you, which I'm guessing is more than he's ever done."

"It was only a trail ride!" Not strictly true, she thought. She'd helped him off with his pants and massaged his bare thighs until he became sexually aroused.

"Whitlock isn't so sure." He peered up at her. "Come to think of it, neither am I."

Freddy took a deep breath. "Believe me, when I planned this, I had no intention of—"

"I know. Neither of us could have known." He gave her a long, assessing look. "As I said, I thought you were a man."

"And I thought you were a big-shot businessman."

"That's exactly what I am."

She shook her head. "You're far more than that," she said softly.

"Thank you."

"You've earned it."

He held her gaze for a moment. "You know I'm going to buy the ranch."

"I know."

"Which will make me your boss."

Her heart beat a quick rhythm. "I know that, too."

The fire in his eyes was a controlled blaze. "I've seen personal involvement ruin a lot of business relationships."

"With your experience, I'm sure you have." Her mouth was as dry as the desert floor. "And I want to be the foreman of the True Love for a very long time."

"Then I guess we put our personal feelings on hold."

"Yes, I guess we do."

6

BY THE TIME they reached the pond, Ry's troubles had shifted from his thighs to his feet. He could see no point in toughing it out for the sake of vanity—Freddy had witnessed one of the more vulnerable moments of his life when she'd applied the Bag Balm to his thighs. So when they reached the water, he tethered Mikey and leaned against the tree to pull off his boots.

"Now you understand why cowboys ride instead of walk," Freddy said.

"I do indeed." Without rolling up the stiff cuffs of his jeans, he waded straight into the water. "Good God!" The icy water immediately numbed his feet, and although he tried to grip the algae-covered rocks with his toes, they refused to cooperate. Arms flailing, he landed on his tender rear. On impact, his hat sailed into the water and he grabbed it just before it floated away like a child's toy boat. He slapped the dripping hat on his head and sat there, too disgusted to move.

Freddy dismounted and sauntered over to the pond. "How's the water?"

She was a real smart aleck, he thought. As he sat and fumed, a plot formed in his mind, a plot born of twelve hours of the most extreme discomfort he had ever remembered. Now his butt was numb, which wasn't all bad, but he'd never immersed his body in such cold water in his life. She'd seen what he was about to do. She could have warned him. Now it was payback time.

"Ry?"

From the corner of his eye, he saw her step closer.

"Are you okay?"

The sudden lunge was excruciatingly painful, but worth it. On the football field, his unsportsmanlike tackle would have earned him a flag, but this wasn't a sanctioned game. In two seconds, Freddy was splashing and sputtering next to him in the water.

"Ry McGuinnes, that was the nastiest, meanest—" She started to struggle to her feet and he grabbed her arm to jerk her back down.

"Leaving so soon, Miss Singleton?" He looked her over and noted with satisfaction that her jeans and shirt were soaked. Her hat had flipped backward onto the embankment and water dripped from the ends of her hair. He held her wrist in an iron grip. "The water isn't too *cold* for you, is it? Since you failed to warn me about it, I assumed you'd want to join me in a little swim."

She glared at him. "My boots will be ruined. And I thought you were a gentleman."

"And I thought you were a lady. A lady would have cautioned me about the cold water and the slippery rocks. A lady wouldn't have taunted me once I fell in." He'd begun to notice something else. Beneath the soaked front of her blouse, her nipples shoved against the material in protest against the chill. Now that he'd given in to the need for revenge, other needs began asserting themselves, as if they'd only required the merest crack in his armor of self-control to slip through.

"I'm only trying to save my ranch!" she protested, her chest heaving.

This dunking was either a very good idea or a very bad one, he thought, longing to unfasten the snaps of her shirt. He looked into her eyes. "And I'm only trying to save my hide," he said pleasantly. She had such beautiful eyes, the same dusky color as the sagebrush growing along the trail.

"Why don't you just give up?" she cried.

"Why don't you?" He studied her expressive mouth. The water was cold as a snowbank, but her mouth would be warm . . . so warm.

"What do you need this ranch for?" Her eyes misted, dew on sage. "Can't you go buy some more pork bellies or something and be just as happy?"

"Not anymore." He reached up and grazed her lower lip with his knuckle. Had she flinched, he would have released her and climbed out of the water. It was definitely the wisest move he could make. But she didn't flinch. Instead, her pupils widened in awareness. He sucked in a breath. "Instead of discouraging me, your behavior has only made me more determined," he said.

Her lashes swept down and pink tinged her cheeks. "To buy the ranch?"

He paused, allowing time for her imagination to work. "That's what we're talking about, isn't it?"

"Of course." She said it too softly for the words to carry any conviction. "Anything else would be a mistake. We already settled that."

"Yes, we did." He slid his damp hand behind her neck and she shivered, but whether from the chill or from anticipation, he couldn't know. "But I thought you weren't going to sabotage me anymore, either."

"That wasn't really sabotage."

"No?"

Her gaze reconnected with his and the turmoil in her eyes betrayed her inner struggle. "Some things just happen."

"So I'm discovering." He guided her closer, watching the battle rage until at last her lashes fluttered down in partial surrender.

Their breath mingled for a long moment as he hesitated. Logic tried for a foothold in his brain and failed. He had to taste her. With the first brush of his lips, her breath hitched, and he knew she was strung as tight as he. Misgivings assaulted him, but the velvet promise of her mouth beckoned. He skimmed over her lips once again and his heart lurched when he discovered them parted in welcome.

Had he imagined anything less from this woman? With a groan, he settled his mouth firmly against hers. And was lost. Her warmth rose to meet him; her passion ignited in concert with his. Her vibrant spirit had led him through hell. Now she offered heaven.

And he took—greedily, angrily, venting hours of frustration with his lips and tongue. She gave without restraint, matching his assault with one of her own. Water sluiced between them as he pulled her close. They might have been naked from the waist up, so drenched were their shirts. His heart pounded as her breasts cushioned the tautness of his chest and he could feel the distinct imprint of her nipples. She wound her arms around his back, pressing, kneading, wanting. Desire defied the icy water as heat spread through him, warming his groin, his thighs, his calves, nibbling on his toes. *Nibbling on his toes?*

He lifted his mouth a fraction. "Do you feel that?"

"Yes." She pressed against him. "Don't stop."

"On your toes?"

"Down to my toes," she agreed, her tone impatient. "Don't talk. Just kiss me like that again."

The nibble came again. "Not *down* to your toes, *on* your toes."

She drew back and frowned. "I have on boots. Two-hundred-dollar boots that may never be the same after this. What are you talking about?"

Ry released her and scrambled to his feet. "Your father's blessed bass! Is every damn thing in this country booby-trapped?"

She sat and stared at him as the sensual haze cleared from her expression and her jaw clenched. "Yes! Yes, it is!" She struggled out of the water, her boots squishing. "Especially to people who don't know the territory. Get that through your thick Yankee head, will you? You don't belong here!"

She'd probably never forgive him for that kiss, he thought. And worse, she'd never forgive herself. He grabbed his boots. "We'll see about that. And by the way, I'm borrowing Maureen for the rest of the trip. This cowboy has walked his last mile."

THEY DIDN'T SPEAK again after that. Which was just as well, Freddy thought as she trudged heavily down the trail toward the ranch's corrals, the wet leather of her boots complaining with every step. Why in heaven's name had she let him kiss her? They could have eventually forgotten about the incident with the Bag Balm, but a kiss was never forgotten. Especially a kiss like that, one that probed deep into the secret canyons of desire they'd kept hidden from each other until now. She was doomed.

Duane was giving a beginning riding lesson in the main corral when they approached. Two men, a woman and two children turned to stare as Freddy led Mikey over to the large metal watering trough. Duane glanced in their direction, pulled his hat lower over his eyes and continued with the lesson. At least he hadn't laughed out loud, and for that she decided to give him a bonus at pay time. If her new bosses would allow it, she thought with a wave of bitterness.

She imagined what she must look like. Eager to end this disastrous trail ride, she'd started down the mountain with her clothes and boots still wet. Along the way, she and Mikey had stirred up the dry dust of the trail, which had caked onto her wet clothes and dried, until she probably looked like an adobe version of a cowgirl.

She held Mikey's reins loosely while he drank. At last, unable to bear the suspense, she flicked a glance back to see if Ry was coming.

He was, slow but sure. Outwardly, he looked better than she did, because he'd at least been riding above the clouds of dust. But the grim set of his mouth told her he wasn't in as good shape as he looked. He walked Maureen over to the trough and let her drink while he stayed in the saddle. Freddy waited for him to climb down. It wasn't nice to stand there waiting for his groan of pain when he dismounted, but in her present frame of mind, she no longer cared about nice. Ry didn't budge.

"Aren't you getting down?" she said at last, unable to contain her curiosity.

He stared straight ahead. "Nope."

"Why not?"

"I think my butt's welded to the saddle."

She bit the inside of her lip to control a chuckle. "I see. Want me to get Duane to help you off?" She figured that would light a fire under him.

It did. He wasn't far wrong about being welded in, though. Moisture, heat and dust had formed something similar to glue between denim and leather. His backside came out of the saddle with a sound like a cow pulling its hoof out of the mud.

Freddy's laughter broke through. She couldn't help it. She'd probably be fired before the day was out, anyway. And once she started laughing, she couldn't stop. She laughed until tears streamed down her mud-caked cheeks.

Ry's bowlegged hobble as he walked over to her made her laugh even harder.

"Think it's pretty funny, do you?" he asked.

She nodded, too overcome with giggles to speak.

He stood there, legs spread and hands on his hips while she gasped and tried to regain her composure, only to have a new fit of hysterics overtake her.

Duane rode over to the edge of the corral. "You got a problem over there?" he called.

"I think she's having a fit," Ry said. "Any suggestions?"

"Nope. Never seen her get like that."

Freddy laughed even harder.

"Only one thing for it," Ry said, coming toward her with his bowlegged swagger.

"Now, Ry," she said, starting to hiccup as she backed away from him.

"This always works in the movies."

He was surprisingly quick, considering his condition. She whooped in protest as he threw her over his shoulder like a sack of feed.

"Put me down!" she screamed, kicking and struggling. But it was too late. Water splashed over her head as he dumped her in the horse trough. After the first shock, it felt surprisingly good and not half as cold as the snow-fed pond. She came up for air slowly and pushed her hair out of her face to find several sets of eyes, including Mikey's and Maureen's, focused on her. The guests seemed fascinated, but Duane looked terrified. He'd never seen anyone toss his foreman in the horse trough before, and he obviously expected all hell to break loose.

Then she glanced at Ry, who was regarding her with his arms crossed over his chest and his gaze enigmatic. She wanted to strangle him for making a spectacle of her. She longed to lash out at him for being a bully and a cad. But the cool water had brought her to her senses. A man who would toss her in the horse trough certainly had enough moxie to clinch a deal on the ranch. That meant he would soon hold her fate in the palm of his hand. And staying on the ranch had always been, and continued to be, the most important thing in the world to her.

She met his gaze. "Thanks," she said sweetly. "I needed that." Then she climbed out of the trough with as much dignity as she could manage, considering she was a walking waterfall. One boot stayed in the trough and she had to fish it out. She poured the water onto the ground, put the boot on and took the other off to repeat the process. Then she reached for her hat floating on the surface of the water and settled it on her head. Water drizzled down her face as if she were standing in the shower. She blew the drops away. "If you'll please unsaddle the horses, I'll go up to the house and change into something dry so I can tend Mikey's wound."

"Be glad to," he said amiably, his blue eyes dancing. There was something deeper burning there, too, something that might have been admiration.

Freddy glanced over at Duane. "Can I borrow your truck?"

"Keys are on the floor," Duane said, looking totally amazed. "Need any help?"

"Not at the moment." Back straight and leaving a dribbling trail of water in the dust, she marched over to Duane's old truck and climbed in.

EAGER TO CALL Joe Gilardini, Ry put off his Jacuzzi and took a quick shower before changing into khaki slacks and a white cotton shirt with the sleeves rolled to the elbow. As physically miserable as he'd been wearing Curtis's and Duane's cowboy garb, he already missed it.

A light snack had been waiting in his room when he'd arrived, probably ordered up by Freddy. She'd apparently had an attitude adjustment since her baptism in the horse trough. Much as he didn't want a continual fight on his hands, he would miss her fiery belligerence.

He ate his food and rehearsed his pitch for bringing Joe into the partnership. Going by the rough figures Joe had given him on the money in his pension fund, the deal could be finalized with that and with what Ry could raise. Lavette would make things easier all the way around, but Joe was the critical part of the transaction.

Yet Joe hadn't been willing to commit himself before Ry had left Manhattan. Over drinks at Joe's favorite bar, the cop had told Ry that yes, he was definitely quitting the force, but no, he wasn't sure a guest ranch was the place to put his retirement money. All he'd promised was that he'd have exact figures on his pension the next time they talked. No promises, no commitment to invest the pension, but he would have the figures.

So this was it. If Joe wouldn't go for the deal, Ry would have to start through his list of contacts until he found someone who'd put up the money. And he'd have to do it fast, before Westridge became tired of waiting and accepted Whitlock's puny offer. In the past twenty-four hours, that possibility had become unacceptable to Ry.

Clearing the tension from his throat, he picked up the receiver of the phone on his bedside table and dialed an outside line. Then he sat on the bed, an antique four-poster, while he punched in Joe's number. As the exchanges clicked through, he gazed out the window. His room was at the corner of the house, with one window facing the mountains and the other looking out on the wide front porch. Holding the receiver to his ear, he walked over to the porch window and leaned against the wall to look out. At the far end of the porch, sitting on one of several old cane-bottomed chairs, was Dexter Grimes, his walker positioned to one side of his chair. Next to him sat Leigh Singleton. A long-haired black-and-white dog rested at their feet, completing the Norman Rockwell portrait.

The line rang, and Joe answered quickly.

"Joe, this is Ry—T. R. McGuinnes. Have you got those figures?"

"Sure." Joe sounded impatient. "But first tell me what the ranch is like."

Ry closed his eyes with relief. He had no idea what had changed Joe's thinking, but from the tone of his voice, the cop was hooked. For the next ten minutes, Ry described the ranch house, the corrals, the horses and the ranch hands, but didn't discuss the True Love curse. He mentioned the John Wayne Room but omitted anything about spiders and scorpions. He described the reservoir stocked with bass but didn't add the story of his personal experience with the fish.

"Have you been out riding?" Joe asked.

"Some," Ry said with a grimace. "There's a beautiful spot above Rogue Canyon where you can see the whole valley."

"Sounds great, just great. What's this guy Freddy Singleton like? Think we can work with him?"

A picture of Freddy coming up out of the horse trough like Venus rising from the sea made Ry smile. "Freddy's a woman," he said. *Is she ever.*

"No joke? Probably one of those leathery old ranch gals, full of vinegar."

His fingers still remembered the softness of her cheek, and his mouth retained the rich taste of her lips. "She's full of vinegar, all right. But she's not what I'd call leathery."

There was a pause on the other end. "Are you telling me that Freddy the foreman is a babe?"

"I wouldn't let her hear you say that, if I were you."

"McGuinnes, you must be the luckiest s.o.b. on the face of the earth. It's not enough that you're out there in God's country. You've stumbled on a ranch with a beautiful woman as its foreman. I suppose she's married, though, probably to the head wrangler or somebody like that."

"No, the head wrangler is her sister, Leigh."

There was a short bark of laughter. "You're putting me on. This is beginning to sound like a fantasy beer commercial."

"Nope. The Singleton women are very real."

"I'm calling Lavette. This'll settle it for him."

"Look, Joe, the women don't have anything to do with anything. If we buy this place, we'll be their employers. We can't—"

"Yeah, yeah, I know. Still, it beats the heck out of dealing with some grizzled old cowpoke, wouldn't you say?"

Ry thought of all Freddy had put him through and wasn't so sure. A grizzled old cowpoke would have simplified this deal considerably. "I suppose," he agreed, mostly to get off the subject. "We have to start putting this offer together if we want to beat out the neighbor who has already made a lowball bid. Can you give me those pension figures now?"

"You bet. Got them right here." Joe read off the amounts and the method of payment.

Cradling the receiver against his shoulder, Ry scribbled the information on a notepad beside the phone. If they closed the deal in thirty days, Joe would have his pay for unused sick leave and vacation by then. Ry could borrow the rest, with Joe making payments out of his monthly pension checks, but a contribution from the trucker would help a lot in the beginning.

"Have you talked with Lavette recently?" Ry asked.

"Yesterday. The doctors can't guarantee he'll be able to continue his trucking career, and the insurance company wants to settle for a lump sum. Personally, I think he should take the money and run. I'll go see him and fill him in on the ranch details. Maybe that'll help him get off the dime."

"Good idea." Ry walked the length of the telephone cord. "Tell me, why are you so gung ho all of a sudden?"

His question was met with silence.

"Hey, if it's too personal, forget it. I'm glad you're on board."

"It's my kid," Joe said, his tone reluctant. "My ex-wife and her new husband are turning him into a pansy."

Ry struggled to connect this information to Joe's decision to go in on the ranch. "And . . . ?"

"And I figure if I bring him out to the ranch, I can toughen him up some."

Ry bit back his laughter. "No doubt. Just turn him over to Freddy Singleton."

"I mean, he's not a complete weenie yet. He's only seven, but I can see where he's headed and I figure it's up to me to turn him around."

Ry decided to play devil's advocate, to make sure Joe was nailed down tight. "But you wouldn't have to buy the place. You could just pay for a week or two as a guest."

"It wouldn't be the same. If Kyle thinks of me as part owner of the spread, I think I have a better chance."

The spread. Ry loved it. Joe was nailed down, all right. Welcome to the Ponderosa, Joe Gilardini. "You may have a point."

"And it's a good investment, right? We'll make a lot of money when we sell it?"

"I don't see how we can lose, Joe."

7

AFTER RY FINISHED his phone call, he felt restless. He couldn't start negotiating with the bankers until morning, although he itched to start putting the deal together. He called his lawyer about drawing up a partnership agreement, but he'd left the office and Ry decided not to bother him at home.

By consulting an activities schedule left on his pine dresser, he discovered dinner didn't begin until six. He had a couple of hours to kill. He walked back into the main room of the ranch house, which was deserted, and surveyed the pool and Jacuzzi. Both were busy. He decided to postpone his soak until evening, when it was more likely nobody would be around.

Then he headed for the front porch, thinking he might take a walk down to the stables and check on Mikey. Everyone else around here drove between the house and the stables, but the distance wasn't any longer than between his office on Wall Street and Battery Park, where he sometimes walked on his lunch break to enjoy the sweep of the harbor and a view of the Statue of Liberty.

"Mr. McGuinnes," a woman called.

He turned.

Leigh Singleton still sat on the far end of the porch. Dexter and his walker were gone, but the dog remained, curled across her feet. "Need a lift somewhere?" she asked.

He walked back in her direction. "Not really. I was headed down to the corrals. I can walk that."

"I'm sure you can," she said with an easy smile. She wore her honey-colored hair caught back in a clip, as Freddy did. Her faded jeans and work shirt spoke of practicality, but she wore silver hoop earrings decorated with an intricate design. A small turquoise feather dangled from each hoop. And her eyes, golden brown and almond-shaped, seemed exceedingly wise for a woman as young as Leigh. "I would have thought you'd had enough exercise for a while," she added.

He flushed. "I'm a little tougher than you and your sister give me credit for."

"Apparently. But if you were hoping to see Freddy down at the corrals, she's not there. After she doctored Mikey, she rode out to check on one of the stock tanks which seems to be leaking."

Of course he'd hoped to see Freddy, he admitted to himself. "I wasn't going down to see her, specifically. I—"

Leigh waved a hand, cutting off his protest. "Any man who spent twenty-four hours with my sister and *wasn't* interested in her would have something wrong with him, don't you think?"

"Depends on whether he's a masochist."

She chuckled. "Freddy's not usually like that. You've threatened her very existence. *Our* very existence, to be exact. Do you blame her for fighting back?"

"I'll probably feel a lot more charitable when my backside returns to normal."

"Yet you were headed down to the corrals because you thought she might be there, doctoring Mikey."

He opened his mouth to deny it, but the all-knowing look in Leigh's eyes made him close it again.

"Care to sit a spell, Mr. McGuinnes?"

"Ry," he said, stepping up on the wooden porch and crossing to the chair next to her.

The dog raised his head, but at a word from Leigh it settled back down. "Ry?" Leigh asked, frowning. "I thought you went by initials. J.R., or TWA, or something."

"Cute. It's T.R."

"I was close. So why the change?"

Then Freddy hadn't told her everything, he thought, gratified. Of course, Freddy might not want anyone to know all the intimate details of their outing. Unless she was a liar, which he sensed she wasn't, she'd have to admit he'd kissed her. Brutal honesty would have required her to add that she'd enjoyed it. "Your sister suggested calling me Ry," he said. "She thought T.R. sounded stuffy."

"Did she?" Leigh gave him an assessing look. "Sounds as if Freddy is somewhat interested, as well. She doesn't assign nicknames to people she doesn't like."

Ry glanced away, afraid those knowing eyes would read too many things from his expression. "If the deal goes through and my partners and I buy the ranch, you and Freddy will become our employees. She and I both understand the politics of that."

Leigh chuckled. "Loosen up, Ry. Out here on the ranch, we don't worry about office politics. People are people. Besides, you don't strike me as the kind who would fire an employee because a love affair didn't work out."

"No, I wouldn't. But she might quit."

"She wouldn't leave the True Love over something like that. But suit yourself. Lord knows, I'm not trying to talk you into anything. I'm glad you decided to take the name she slapped on you, though."

He shrugged and stretched out his legs. The gesture hurt like hell, but he was working hard to appear nonchalant. "No big deal." He wished he had on denim and boots. Out here in the West, denim and boots seemed to telegraph nonchalance much faster than khakis and deck shoes. "I'm pretty burned out with the big-city routine. The new name felt right." He looked over at her. "This ranch feels right."

"You're not the first person to think so. The True Love has been welcoming people home for generations."

Ry straightened in his chair. "That's going a bit further than I intended. I'm just talking about a change of pace. Nothing permanent."

"Oh, I see." She sat quietly, gazing out across the sparse crop of grass.

"What are those earrings supposed to be?" he asked. "They look like a special design."

She reached up to finger one of the silver hoops. "They're called dream catchers. Indian legend has it that the web keeps bad dreams out and lets good ones through."

"What's your take on this curse business?"

She turned those incredible almond-shaped eyes on him. "When something as terrible as that massacre happens, the land bears the mark of it, whether it was deliberately cursed or not. But I like to think the Singletons have been pumping good vibrations into the area for so many generations that the power of the curse is fading." She smiled at him. "After all, Thaddeus Singleton did name it the True Love. Think of the energy inherent in that."

"Energy in a name? Come on, Leigh."

She gazed at him, her sense of inner calm almost palpable. "I can't believe you would doubt it . . . Ry."

He gazed at her as a chill ran up his spine. He'd assumed he could buy this ranch, change its name, revamp its purpose and move on, a wealthier man. Why did that assumption seem suddenly naive?

Leigh nudged the dog from her feet and stood. "If you'll excuse me, I have to drive down to the corrals and saddle a few trail horses. We have a sunset ride scheduled tonight." She glanced down at him. "Want to come on the ride?"

"I—ah—"

She laughed. "Never mind. I was teasing you. Besides, you'd probably better stay here. Last I heard, Freddy had called Eb Whitlock and invited him to have supper in our dining room with her and the other guests, as a gesture of thanks for his coming up to check on you two this morning. You'll probably want to hang around and protect your interests."

He lifted his eyebrows.

"In the ranch, of course," she explained. Then, with a low whistle to the dog, she cut across the yard to yet another battered pickup with the ranch's brand painted on the door panel. This truck boasted an added decoration, however. Over its dark blue fender curved an iridescent rainbow.

FREDDY TOLD HERSELF she'd invited Eb out of courtesy. After all, he had gone out of his way this morning to make sure she was okay. But her pride still smarted from that dunking in the horse trough. She wasn't above needling Ry a little with Eb's presence at her dinner table.

With only eleven guests in residence and five of them out on a sunset trail ride and barbecue, the dining room seemed almost empty. The six remaining guests had all been at the ranch for a week and had become friends, so they commandeered one of the longer pine tables. Freddy ushered Eb to a table set for four with the traditional True Love heart-shaped place mats in red-and-white checks, red napkins and tin plates enameled in red with white flecks.

"I see you've kept the traditions alive," Eb commented, pulling out a chair for Freddy.

"With difficulty." Freddy kept glancing at the door to see if Ry would appear for dinner. "This tinware isn't easy to find anymore."

Eb leaned forward as he pushed her chair closer to the table, and she could feel his breath on her bare shoulders. Her blouse, one Leigh had talked her into buying, had "cold-shoulder" cutouts. The blouse, along with a tiered denim skirt, was her newest outfit, and she'd swept her hair on top of her head and added silver concho earrings. She hadn't been this dressed up in weeks. But a woman who had last appeared climbing from a horse trough had to think of her image.

Of course, Ry might skip dinner. At this moment, he could easily be sound asleep in his room. At least he wasn't in the Jacuzzi—she'd checked.

"I *said*, this sure brings back memories," Eb said, a little too loudly and with a trace of impatience.

Freddy realized she hadn't heard him the first time. "Yes, it does." She smiled at Eb, who had seated himself at right angles to her. "Sorry I haven't had you over sooner, but . . ."

"Never mind. I know you've had troubles. Seems like all sorts of things have been going wrong."

Although he hadn't touched her, Freddy felt crowded. She'd never realized how Eb seemed to gobble space. "Just a little bad luck is all, Eb."

Manny, one of only two waiters they kept on during the summer months, came by the table with a trayful of salad plates. "Just the two of you at this table, Miss Singleton?"

Freddy sincerely hoped not. She'd invited Eb as a little dig at Ry, but now she was in danger of spending the meal alone with her silver-haired neighbor. Both Leigh's and Ry's assessments of Eb had been weighing on her mind. "I'm not sure, Manny. Why don't you leave another salad, just in case?"

Eb glanced at her. "Isn't Leigh out on a sunset trail ride?"

"Yes."

His expression of goodwill dimmed. "Then I guess you must be expecting your prospective buyer," he said. "Before he arrives, we need to talk. I was hoping your trail ride would discourage him."

"So was I, but he doesn't discourage easily."

Manny put salads in front of both of them. "Where would you like the third one?" he asked.

Eb patted the place mat beside him at the same moment Freddy pointed to the seat next to her. Manny paused as he looked from Eb to Freddy.

"Here, I'll take that from you," Ry said, sitting down next to Freddy. "You look lovely tonight," he murmured to her.

"Thank you." The compliment filled her with pleasure, far too much pleasure for her own good.

"So, McGuinnes, you survived," Eb said.

"So I did. How are you doing, Whitlock?" He reached across the table to shake Eb's hand. "How's Gold Digger?"

"Gold Strike," Eb corrected.

"Oh, yeah." Ry grinned. "You'll have to forgive me. I'm new around here."

"So I noticed. I was wondering how you found your way to the table without a maître d'." Eb gave Ry a wide smile that looked totally insincere.

"We city dwellers learn to be resourceful. I just followed the light flashing off your bolo tie, Eb. May I call you Eb? I'll bet you need a winch to hoist that hunk of silver over your head every morning."

Eb's smile disappeared. "I'm surprised to see you up and about, McGuinnes, much less cracking jokes."

"Yeah, me, too." Ry hoisted his water glass in Freddy's direction. "To the power of . . . youth."

Freddy knew she shouldn't be enjoying this, but Eb was always so darn full of himself that it was fun to watch someone pricking his balloon of self-importance. In the next moment, she felt guilty. During her father's illness, Eb had almost made a pest of himself with offers to help out. Once, he'd graded the road to the ranch without asking and another time he'd rounded up several of her strays who'd wandered through a break in the fence, returned the cattle and mended the fence. Freddy had been grateful, but Leigh had contended he was building up points toward some future goal.

"I suppose Freddy's told you about the curse on this place," Eb said between bites of salad.

"She has. Fortunately, I'm not a superstitious man."

Freddy glanced at Eb in surprise. "You don't believe in the True Love curse, do you?"

"I didn't used to." Eb pushed away his empty salad plate. "But consider the run of bad luck you've had recently, Freddy. First your father's cancer. Then you were forced to sell to this big-shot corporation, but the place still hasn't turned a profit. Maybe there's something to that curse business. Even a relatively minor thing like Mikey getting cut up, or your stock tank springing a leak. And remember, too, that calf was stillborn, and pack rats chewed the wiring in two of your trucks."

"Pack rats and stock-tank leaks are just part of living out here in the desert, Eb," Freddy said, irritated by his catalog of mishaps.

"Don't happen that much to me." Eb leaned back in his chair and puffed out his chest.

Or you keep quiet if they do, Freddy thought, and felt uncharitable for thinking it.

Manny replaced the salad plates with servings of T-bone, baked potatoes and beans.

Ry picked up his steak knife. "If I didn't know better, Whitlock, I'd say you're trying to scare me off so you can buy this place for a song. Not that I blame you," he added, cutting into his steak. "Any good businessman would try the same thing."

"Oh, I'm no businessman," Eb said, with a sly nudge of Freddy's knee under the table. "I'm just a rancher."

Freddy felt like a dope. Of course Eb was trying to discourage Ry with all this talk of the ranch's curse. In his typical heavy-handed way, he was trying to help. And she would prefer that Eb buy the place, wouldn't she?

Manny returned to the table. "Excuse me, but there's a call for Mr. McGuinnes."

Ry looked up, his expression alight with anticipation. He turned to Freddy. "Where can I take it?"

"You can go in my office. Just head straight across the main room. The door's open."

After Ry left, Eb heaved a sigh. "I do hate city slickers. I'm surprised he didn't whip out one of those cellular jobs."

"Eb, I thought you just bought one of those things?"

Eb looked uncomfortable. "Okay, I did, but it's just to take out on the range. You should get one, too. It used to be safe for women to ride around this country alone, but not anymore..." He peered in the direction Ry had taken. "Any type of idiot could be out there."

"He's turned out to have spunk, Eb," Freddy said. "I know he's a greenhorn, but he took that trail ride like a man."

Eb gave her a sharp look. "You changing your mind about city guys buying the place?"

"No, not really. Westridge was bad enough, but at least they left me in charge. I have the distinct impression these men wouldn't do that."

"Bet your bottom dollar on it. This McGuinnes is a real wheeler-dealer. He—" Eb didn't finish the sentence as Ry came back into the dining room.

His walk was still a little bowed, and he still grimaced as he sat down, but his blue eyes glowed as he looked at Freddy. "Good news. My third partner is definitely in."

The leap of excitement in her chest caught her totally by surprise.

"And just what does that mean?" Eb asked.

Ry looked across the table at him. "That it's a done deal, neighbor."

FOR THE REST of the meal, Freddy felt like a referee at a sporting event. Eb paraded his knowledge about ranching and Ry parried the rancher's boasting with thrusts of razor-sharp wit. By the time Eb said his goodbyes and drove away in his king-cab dual-wheel pickup, she would gladly have carried him to his ranch on her back.

"Lovely evening," Ry said as he stood next to her on the porch.

She shot him a sideways glance. "I suppose you enjoyed yourself."

"You bet."

"Men," she muttered, lifting her gaze heavenward. "By the way, what are these two partners of yours like?"

He shoved his hands into his pockets. "You know, this is the craziest deal I've ever put together, with the most unlikely characters. A trucker, a New York City cop and me. Can you imagine a stranger combination than that?"

She was unwillingly intrigued. "How did you ever link up with them?"

"We were all in the same elevator accident."

Her stomach pitched. "Were you hurt?" she asked before she could stop herself, before the betraying note of concern could be banished from her question.

He gazed at her, a smile of irony making a brief appearance. "A minor concussion, which is nothing compared to the way I've been battered since I arrived here."

Freddy avoided his gaze. "What about the other two?"

"My briefcase went flying and gashed open the cop's chin, and he also broke his arm. The trucker hurt his back, which put his trucking career in jeopardy but gave him a nice settlement. The cop's quitting the force and sinking his pension into the ranch."

She stared at him in disbelief. "You're using an insurance settlement and someone's retirement fund to buy the ranch?"

"Along with every asset of mine I could liquefy."

"Doesn't that worry you, risking people's nest eggs?"

"No. People thrive on risk. It's playing it safe that ruins them. These two men were both stagnating, needing a challenge but not sure what it should be. I provided one."

From his assured tone of voice, Freddy easily pictured him in a luxurious office in Manhattan, playing the market with nerves of steel, winning and losing small fortunes as if he were using Monopoly money. "And what about you? Did you need a challenge, too?"

"Apparently, I did."

"I suppose your partners will want to come out to the ranch, too."

"Definitely. Chase Lavette, the trucker, plans a trip as soon as the physical therapists have released him, and Joe, the cop, wants to bring his little boy out."

"Of course, the deal isn't finalized," she said. "It could still fall through somehow, or one of your partners could back out."

"They won't."

As crickets chirped in the mesquite branches, Freddy turned this new information over in her mind. She'd been devastated when she'd had to sell the ranch to Westridge, but life around the True Love hadn't changed as much as she'd expected. This time, however, the owners wouldn't be a faceless company. Real people were buying the True Love, people looking for a challenge. God knows what havoc that could create. She felt a headache coming on. "Maybe it's time to call it a day," she said. "We probably both could use some rest."

"Should I check for bugs before I go to bed?"

"No," she said with a weary shake of her head. "We're on a regular schedule with an efficient exterminator. You're safe here."

"I'm almost sorry to hear that."

She looked into his eyes. Had he already developed a taste for danger?

"Good night, Freddy," he said softly. "Sleep well."

Nodding, she retreated inside before the spark of excitement in his gaze could lure her to stay.

TWO HOURS LATER, her headache was worse. Climbing out of bed, she changed into her red tank-style bathing suit, grabbed a towel and headed toward the pool. But once she'd entered the enclosed patio, she paused. Ry was in the Jacuzzi, his head pillowed on a towel, his eyes closed.

She decided to go back to her room, but for a moment she stood and watched him. His arms were stretched out along the lip of the Jacuzzi and his broad chest moved rhythmically as warm water foamed and splashed against his taut belly. Droplets of water clinging to the pelt of his chest hair winked in the light from a nearby gas lantern. Desire eddied through her, but it wasn't just the sight of his naked torso that stirred her senses. It wasn't even the memory of his kiss, although that played a part. But physical beauty and sensuality wouldn't have captured her imagination if she hadn't witnessed the courage with which he'd faced whatever trials she'd thrown at him since his arrival yesterday. He'd responded just like . . . a cowboy.

Perhaps he'd make a good owner of the ranch, after all. But he would be the owner, and he didn't believe in compromising his business relationships with personal involvement. She thought it was a wise strategy, herself. She turned to leave the patio.

"Don't go."

She stopped in midstride.

"I owe you an apology."

She swung back, astonished. "*You* owe *me* an apology? How do you figure?"

He'd lifted his head from the towel and gazed at her. "I lost control at least twice today. I shouldn't have dunked you in the horse trough, for one thing."

"I probably had it coming." Her heart pummeled her ribs. "Nobody likes to be laughed at."

He gave her a wry grin. "That doesn't excuse my assaulting you . . . in the pond."

She wondered if he considered the tackle an assault, or the kiss. Whichever it was, she didn't think they were wise to discuss the incident. "Never mind. I don't hold grudges."

"Good. Because I have a favor to ask." He braced his hands on the edge of the Jacuzzi and lifted himself upward, so he sat with only his feet dangling in the water. His trunks were very brief and very wet. "I noticed you have a fax in your office. I'd like to use it in the morning, if you don't mind. I'll cover the charges."

Freddy gulped and glanced away. "No problem. I have some errands to run in Tucson tomorrow, so I won't be working in there, anyway."

"I see. If my being out here now makes you uncomfortable, I'll go in and let you have the patio to yourself," he said.

She focused on his face and tried to ignore the Chippendale image he presented lounging on the lip of the Jacuzzi. "That's ridiculous."

"I agree. We can't work together very well if you run every time I show up."

"I wasn't—"

"You would have left the patio if I hadn't called you back." He got to his feet. "Do you want the hot tub? I'm ready for a swim."

The last thing she needed was warm, swirling water to stir her senses even more. "I was planning on a swim, myself."

"Think we can share the pool?"

"Of course." She tossed her towel on a chaise, took the pins from her hair and executed a shallow dive into the illuminated water. The cool shock of the water was like a brisk slap in the face, one she probably needed. She swam under the surface to the deep end and glided up beside the diving board. She glanced around to locate Ry, and her breath caught. He stood in the arch behind the waterfall like some Polynesian god, the golden accent lights caressing his muscles as he braced for the dive, pushed cleanly through the cascading water and jack-knifed into the pool.

He came up next to her, his hair darkened with water, his eyes seeming to mirror the turquoise blue of the pool. "Want to race?"

She'd do anything that would distract her from the sight of his virile body. "Okay."

"Four lengths of the pool. I'll give you a head start."

"Nothing doing."

"I should have guessed." He hooked both hands over the side and faced the shallow end. She followed suit. "On three," he said. "One, two, *three!*"

Freddy pushed off, but his counting reminded her of pulling his pants off, which reminded her of massaging ointment into his thighs, which reminded her of what she was trying so hard to forget. She swam, determined to break the languorous hold of her forbidden passions. He pulled ahead, and she redoubled her efforts. She'd taken trophies in school for the Australian crawl.

But she was racing an athlete, she remembered, as he lengthened his lead. And what did it matter, this silly race? After it was over, she could go inside, having proven she could handle close encounters of the sensual kind with Ry McGuinnes.

On his last lap, near the middle of the pool, he went down. She saw the water close over his head and immediately thought he'd had a leg cramp. It would be logical after all he'd been through today. Concerned, she dived for the bottom, following the trail of bubbles. The pool was nine feet deep near the drain. He could drown if she weren't here to haul him out.

She reached him and grabbed his shoulders. He grabbed back and pulled her toward him. She struggled, thinking he was going to drown them both. She wasn't strong enough to break away. He drew her closer, despite her efforts to push him back. Then, just before their bodies entwined, she saw his smile.

Light-headed from lack of breath, she held on as he wrapped his arms around her waist and pushed from the bottom of the pool. As they shot upward, he captured her mouth in a dizzying kiss of conquest.

They burst to the surface, and he threw back his head but didn't release her. She gulped in air just before they slipped beneath the water again and he reclaimed her, thrusting his tongue deep into her mouth. The liquid kiss as they sank to the bottom of the pool made her mind spin and her body thump with need. Sanity deserted her and she wrapped her legs around his hips to press shamelessly against his arousal.

This time when he pushed them to the surface, he kept one arm around her and used the other to maneuver them to the side of the pool.

"You're crazy," she whispered, starting to disentangle her legs.

"You're right." One arm anchored them to the side of the pool, the other kept her close. His blue gaze burned into hers. "You're absolutely right."

Her heart thundered in her ears. "And I'm as bad as you are."

"You looked beautiful tonight. Was that for me?" When she didn't answer, his gaze searched hers. "I keep trying to put you out of my mind, Freddy, but then I see you again, looking so kissable, and all my resolutions go out the window."

She could barely breathe. "But we agreed this would be a mistake."

He tightened his grip. "Then why does it feel so right to hold you?"

Her resistance ebbed as her body melded with his. "You should let me go," she whispered.

"I know." He leaned closer for another kiss.

A cough from the shadows invaded the sensual mood. "What was that?" Freddy asked, her eyes probing the area around the pool.

"I didn't hear anything."

"Well, I did." She pushed him gently away. "And even if I didn't, someone could come along at any time."

He reached for her. "Then we'll go somewhere more private."

"No." She was in control again. "You were right when you said we shouldn't get involved. It's too risky . . . for both of us."

The flame slowly faded in his blue eyes and he sighed. "Then I guess you'd better go in. For obvious reasons, I'm staying in the water a while longer."

Her arms trembled as she hoisted herself out of the water. Without looking back, she retrieved her towel and hairpins, slipped into her sandals and left the patio. She'd done some difficult things in her life, and leaving Ry tonight ranked up there as one of the toughest choices she'd ever made.

8

FREDDY DIDN'T show up at breakfast the next morning. If she was deliberately trying to avoid him, he probably deserved it after that stunt in the pool. He'd never before felt the pull of a sensual attraction that completely robbed him of reason. His need for Freddy was disorienting.

After breakfast he walked into her office, half hoping she'd be there, but she wasn't. Last night, he'd been too excited about Lavette's call to take much notice of the office, but now he cast his eyes around the cubicle, intrigued by the little space. The room looked like a converted storage closet; the battered oak desk and chair might have been commandeered from an elementary-school teacher. The same went for the gray metal file cabinet. A computer, a goosenecked lamp and a telephone sat on the desk, and the fax machine occupied the only other piece of furniture in the room, a low bookcase stuffed with ledgers. The room was windowless, which was probably just as well. A window would have taken up too much wall space. Everything in the room spoke of practicality—except for the rogues' gallery on the walls.

The paneling was crammed with framed pictures, each of them a segment of ranch history. A recent color glossy of Leigh on Red Devil nudged against a grainy shot of the old frame ranch house, the surface of the photo cracked and one edge singed. Ry wondered if it had been hastily rescued during the fire Freddy had talked about. Beneath the ranch house picture, women wearing bobbed hair from the twenties posed by the fireplace, and beside that was a portrait of Freddy at about three years of age mounted on a barrel. A closer look showed that the barrel was suspended by ropes. Even at three, she was learning how to ride a bucking bronco.

Ry smiled. All decked out in boots, fringed shirt and hat, Freddy sat straight on the barrel, a wide grin on her face. Ry recognized that grin, the same one she'd given him as they'd raced side by side down the wash two days earlier. It was an expression of pure joy, and he'd felt it, too. Felt it and become frightened. That kind of joy shared with another human being made a person vulnerable to the worst hurt in the world.

He turned from the wall of pictures, walked behind the desk and put his briefcase on its uncluttered surface. Work was the best antidote he'd ever found to that kind of pain. Yet there on the desk, as if to mock him, was a calendar open to May 24, today's date.

The anniversary of Linda's death.

It always ambushed him like a cowardly street thug. Last week, he'd known it was coming, had even realized he'd be in Arizona when it hit. But calendar days didn't seem so important on the ranch, and he'd lost track. That he'd forgotten seemed an act of disloyalty.

Linda would have been the first to criticize him for clinging to his grief. He thought it was the other way around. Grief clung to him like a leech, except when he lost himself in the intense world of commodities trading. And except when he was here. Perhaps that was the magic of this place. Maybe the ranch was the poultice that would draw the agony from him at last.

Well, he'd never know unless he finished putting the deal together. He looked for a wastebasket to rid himself of the piece of paper crumpled in his fist. Then he opened his fingers slowly and stared at the ball of paper. Carefully he pulled it back into shape and grimaced. Without realizing it, he'd torn the page from Freddy's desk calendar. She'd scribbled a couple of things on it—"auto parts" on the first half and "Dexter" on the second. Ry wondered how he'd explain his unthinking vandalism. He'd have to come up with some logical reason.

Stuffing the calendar page into his pocket, he started to pull the chair up to the desk. That was when he first noticed the pillow on the seat. Not a seat cushion, something that might reasonably be on the chair, but a bed pillow, still in its pillowcase.

He wondered who had put it there, and if it was an act of compassion or a taunt. He picked it up and sniffed the case. Freddy's scent, faintly floral, lingered. That devil-woman had taken a pillow from her bed and placed it on her desk chair, expecting him to find it and be reminded that he was a greenhorn who didn't belong here! This was no act of compassion. This was an act of war. His first instinct was to toss the pillow across the room. But, sad to say, he could use the extra padding, although he wasn't as sore today as he had been the day before. He plumped the pillow and settled into the chair. Then he picked up the telephone to begin his business day.

With his first call, he instructed his lawyer to draw up a partnership agreement. Then he spent the rest of the morning haggling with loan officers about interest rates.

Freddy didn't reappear at lunch, either, so Ry used the office again that afternoon when the eager real estate agent arrived at the True Love with the offer typed and ready for Ry's signature. The agent would send the papers to Joe in the overnight mail, and Joe would hand-deliver them to Chase Lavette before shipping them back to Tucson.

Once Ry had put everything in motion toward acquiring the ranch, he sat at the desk tapping the surface with his pen. He had a decision to make. His plane left the next afternoon, and technically he no longer needed to stay in Arizona. The real estate agent would forward the offer to Westridge. Assuming the company accepted it, the closing wouldn't take place for at least two weeks, maybe longer, depending on how efficiently the paper shufflers did their jobs.

But Ry didn't want to go back to New York.

Illogical though it seemed, he felt as if he needed to be physically on the True Love to guarantee the sale. His possessiveness grew with each hour he spent there, almost as if he'd planted a flag in the ground in the same way homesteaders had during the Oklahoma Land Rush.

Besides, now that his butt was healing, he was ready to get back on a horse and toughen himself up. He wanted some jeans and boots of his own to ride in, and he wanted to inspect the ranch in more detail, including the cattle.

And then there was Freddy. He had to figure out how to deal with her. He shouldn't have kissed her again. So what if they were attracted to each other? She didn't want a relationship any more than he did. Romantic involvement would be messy now and possibly disastrous in a couple of years, when the partnership sold the ranch.

Ry was already thinking of ways to soften the blow with better retirement plans for the older employees and financial backing for Freddy and Leigh if they wanted to purchase another ranch. But he wasn't about to buy trouble by announcing those plans now. He just wanted an amiable working relationship with the foreman of his ranch, a relationship that would guarantee a smooth transition when the time came to bring in the developers.

Duane stuck his head in the office doorway, his chewing tobacco making a bulge in his lower lip. "Freddy's not back yet?"

"I haven't seen her."

"Okeydoke." Duane turned away.

"Want to leave her a message?"

Duane swung back, as if Ry had offered a brilliant solution. "I could do that." His smile revealed tobacco-stained teeth. "Leigh asked me to report on Mikey, is all. Looks like he ain't got no infection or nothin'."

Ry tore a fresh sheet of paper from the legal pad he'd been using for his figures and began scribbling a note to Freddy. "That's great news."

"Leigh wanted me to tell Freddy she was goin' over to Whitlock's to practice team ropin'."

Ry wrote that down, too. As long as he was the messenger boy, he might as well do a complete job.

"She has to go over to Eb Whitlock's, 'cause our arena still needs repairs, but you don't have to put that in the note. Freddy knows that."

"Okay." Ry finished the note, smiling at Duane's obvious enjoyment at having someone take dictation from him.

"See, they was waitin' until somebody bought the place before they asked about gettin' the arena fixed. 'Course, some of the guests been askin' about the rodeo and all, but—"

"The *what?*" Ry glanced up.

"We used to have us a rodeo a few times a year, with some easy events for the guests, if they wanted."

Ry's gut reaction was excitement. Rodeo! Then his business sense kicked in as he thought of the liability. "But now you don't?"

Duane looked hopeful. "We can start again, once the arena's in good shape. We kept the *corrientes*, the steers we use just for ropin'." He adjusted his hat and used his tongue to nudge the chewing tobacco to the other side of his lip. "We was hopin' the new owner would take an interest."

"Did anybody tell you the next owner will probably be me?"

"Well, I figured that. Figured it wouldn't hurt none to speak up about the rodeo, neither. The hands like it. I like it, matter of fact."

Ry felt gratified that Duane accepted him enough to tell him all this, but there was no way the True Love would continue holding rodeos. "Did any of the guests ever get hurt?"

"Their pride, mostly. I think we had one broken arm, and a few sprained ankles. That's the guests I'm talkin' about. We always made 'em sign papers sayin' it ain't the ranch's fault."

"Mmm." Such papers wouldn't hold up a minute if someone died or became permanently injured, he thought.

"The hands git hurt all the time, but they ride hurt, anyways. They don't know any other way of doin' things."

Ry nodded, almost in envy. What he really wanted, stupid as it sounded, was to trade places with one of those hands for a while.

"Ever thought about ridin' a bull?" Duane asked.

Adrenaline shot through him. "You have Brahma bulls at this rodeo of yours?"

"A few. Some of the ranchers 'round here like to keep 'em. Eb Whitlock's got a big one that's never been rode. He's called Grateful Dead, 'cause when you get outta the ring, you're grateful you ain't dead."

Ry could almost taste the danger. And he was far too drawn to it. Better to switch topics. "Duane, where's the best place to pick up some Western clothes?"

"I always like the Buckle Barn. The stuff's not too fancy, but it works good."

"In Tucson?"

"Why, no, it's down the road a piece, in La Osa."

"A shopping mall?"

Duane laughed so hard he almost swallowed his chaw. "I reckon not," he said at last, gaining control of himself. "It's a little town, La Osa is. 'Bout ten miles northwest."

What the hell, Ry thought. Might as well go exploring. "Would it be possible to borrow a truck or something, so I can drive there?"

Duane scratched his chin. "Well, now, I can't think of what you could take. My truck's tore apart, waitin' for the new carburetor Freddy's bringin' from town. Leigh's left already, and she borrowed Freddy's truck 'cause hers needs a new fan belt, which Freddy's also bringin', and Freddy's got the van. There's the stove-up vehicles the hands drive, but I'd be real reluctant to put you in one of them. You could break down, easy. Now, if Freddy was to come back, you could—"

"Did I hear my name?" Freddy appeared in the doorway, a leather purse over her shoulder and a plastic bag in one hand. For the trip to town she'd worn denim shorts and a True Love Guest Ranch T-shirt. Her hair was caught up in a ponytail, and instead of a hat, she'd worn sunglasses, which were pushed to the top of her head now that she was indoors. Ry tried not to stare at the graceful curve of her thighs. With her face flushed from the heat and her informal outfit, she looked like a teenager—a very sexy teenager.

She flicked a glance his way and nodded. "Hello."

"Hello." He hoped his casual greeting fooled her. Had he imagined he'd be able to create an amiable working relationship with a woman who affected him the way Freddy did? One look into the sage-colored coolness of her eyes and he longed to replace that indifference with the hot passion he'd seen there the night before. His hand trembled slightly as he closed his briefcase.

"Here's the fan belt and the carburetor," Freddy said, handing Duane the plastic bag. "Let's hope that's all that has to be fixed for now."

"Let's hope." Duane tilted his head toward Ry. "He wants to go to the Buckle Barn, git him some clothes. Should I gas up the van for him?"

Freddy looked at Ry with raised eyebrows. "You want some Western clothes to take back to New York?"

So she remembered that his plane left tomorrow. She was obviously eager for him to be on it. "Something like that."

"I promised Dexter we'd take him to La Osa this afternoon for an ice-cream sundae," she said. "It's a ritual we have once a week, so I can't loan you the van, but you can ride along."

It wasn't the most gracious invitation he'd ever had, but he'd decided he needed to see La Osa. Anything that might impact on the True Love was important, and he hadn't even known of the existence of a little town near the ranch. If it was quaint enough, it might be a selling point for developers. "Sure, that would be great."

"If you're going, you should know a few things about Dexter," she said. "Because of his stroke, he has aphasia. He understands everything you say to him perfectly, but he can't always find the right word to respond. Some people make the mistake of thinking they can talk in front of him as if he weren't there. But he picks up on everything."

"Boy, ain't that the truth," Duane said. "I think he's sharper now than ever. He can hear better than I can."

"I'll keep that in mind," Ry said.

"Meet you out front in fifteen minutes, then," Freddy said, turning.

"Freddy?"

She glanced back at him.

"The pillow was a nice touch."

Her gaze challenged his. "I didn't want you to be uncomfortable today."

"I feel as if I've been cradled in the lap of luxury. In fact, I feel so much better, I'd like you to take me on another ride this evening and show me more of the spread." God, he was doing it again, looking for excuses to be alone with her. He couldn't seem to stop himself.

"I wouldn't advise that," she said in a superior tone that maddened him. "You'll just stiffen up again. If Duane fixes Leigh's truck, we can drive."

"I'd rather ride."

She shrugged. "If you insist. You're the boss."

"Not yet."

"No, but I'm certain you will be."

"Until then, you're still free to tell me to go to hell."

"Only a foolish woman would do that, Mr. McGuinnes." She turned on her heel and left.

Duane gazed after her. "Seems like she's still a little upset 'bout that horse-trough dunkin'."

Ry didn't think it was that at all, but he couldn't very well confide in Duane about the kisses in the pool. "You could be right," he said.

But Duane wasn't right, Ry thought when he climbed into the van fifteen minutes later. Freddy was all smiles for Dexter, who was ensconced in the seat next to her. With Ry, she was coldly polite. It should have been a turnoff, but instead he found her frosty behavior challenging.

"We'll drop you off at the Buckle Barn," she said over her shoulder as she pulled away from the ranch house. "It takes us about thirty minutes to finish our ice cream. Then we'll come back for you."

"Okay."

"What's he want?" Dexter asked Freddy in a surprisingly deep voice for someone so frail.

Ry leaned forward to answer, but Freddy beat him to it.

"Everything, I guess," she said. "You know these Easterners."

"Yeah," Dexter agreed with a chuckle. Then he glanced at Freddy and made a kissing sound. "Last night. In the pool."

So he'd been the one who'd coughed and ended the interlude, Ry thought.

Color climbed into Freddy's cheeks. "That was an unfortunate mistake, Dexter. I was hoping nobody saw that."

"I did," Dexter said.

Freddy's cheeks glowed. "It won't happen again," she said through clenched teeth.

"Blame me, Dexter," Ry said. "I tricked her. She hated every minute of it."

"Nope, she didn't," Dexter said cheerfully.

Freddy groaned. "Dexter, I'd count it the biggest personal favor in the world if you would keep what you saw last night to yourself. Mr. McGuinnes is in the process of buying the True Love, and behavior like last night's doesn't reflect well on either of us."

"Why?"

"We're in a business relationship, that's why."

"Seems okay to me." Dexter pointed to Freddy's left hand. "You don't have one of those things. What are those things?"

"A ring?" she suggested.

"That's it. A ring." His face twisted into a scowl. "Remember that guy? Tried to—clap—no—you know." He smacked his lips again. "To Belinda. She has a ring. Mine."

"Eb didn't mean anything by it, Dexter, really. He kissed her on the cheek because she'd baked him his favorite pie."

"Yeah!" Dexter blustered. "Why'd she do that? She shouldn't do that."

Freddy shook her head and grinned at him. "She was being a good neighbor. You are such a jealous husband."

"Have to be," Dexter said. "Belinda's so easy—no—funny—no. What is it? What is it, Freddy? You know."

"Pretty," Freddy supplied.

"Yeah, pretty. Belinda's pretty. I gotta watch. All the time. Watch that guy."

Ry was so fascinated with the concept that Dexter was still protecting his interests after fifty-some years of marriage that he didn't notice they were in La Osa until Freddy swung the truck off the road and into a dirt parking lot. Not that there was much to notice. La Osa was little more than a wide place in the road with three buildings on the right and three on the left.

He rolled back the side door of the van. "Thanks for the lift."

She glanced at him, her sunglasses disguising her expression. "You're welcome. We'll be back in a half hour."

He consulted his watch. "Fine." Then he climbed down and closed the van's side door. As Freddy backed around and pulled onto the road, he took inventory of La Osa.

A giant soft-ice-cream cone angled out over the parking area of a glass-fronted building at the far end of the street. Obviously the ice-cream parlor. Next to it a large tin-roofed structure was, according to the sign attached to the porch roof, Gonzales's Feed And Hardware Store. Above the sign, a life-size statue of a white horse stood on the flat porch roof. Not just a horse, Ry noticed, but a stallion. The horse's gender had been emphasized by some midnight artist who had painted the stallion's private parts bright blue. The third business on the far side of the street was a two-pump gas station.

On Ry's side of the street stood the Buckle Barn, and next to it a low-slung restaurant that promised live country music, well drinks at a dollar each and "The Biggest T-Bone West of the Pecos." The last business on the strip, looking new and distinctly out of place, was a video store. It was probably the only establishment that would survive once the housing development went in, he thought. The pickup trucks parked nose first in front of each establishment would be replaced by Saabs and BMWs. People who drove those kinds of cars wanted a different type of restaurant, a different kind of ice-cream parlor and no feed store whatsoever.

He mounted the wooden steps to the Buckle Barn, barely glancing at the mannequins in the display windows. He had no time for window-shopping today. The scent of leather greeted him as he walked in the door and headed for the rows of boots standing on shelves against one wall. He was one of only two customers in the store, and within twenty minutes he'd found a pair of elkskin boots soft as a glove, three pairs of brushed-denim boot-cut jeans that molded perfectly to his thighs, and six Western shirts in various patterns and colors. He slipped into a dressing room, put on one pair of jeans, a shirt and the boots before he went in search of the final item, the most personal item, a hat.

WHEN RY WASN'T standing outside the Buckle Barn waiting for her, Freddy decided to go in after him. "Just sit tight," she instructed Dexter, who was looking sleepy after his weekly hot-fudge sundae binge. "I'll go fetch that greenhorn."

Dexter smiled lazily. "Aw, you like him."

"For God's sake, don't say anything like that around him, okay, Dex?" Usually, Freddy treasured Dexter's refreshing honesty. It was as if his stroke had stripped life to the essentials and he wasn't capable of lies, not even little white ones. But now he was exposing emotions she wanted to conceal, especially from herself.

"It's okay," Dexter said, pointing to her left hand again. "No ring."

"It's not that simple." She was losing patience. "He's leaving for New York tomorrow, so that will be the end of that. With any luck, he'll be an absentee landlord like Westridge and I'll never see him again."

"Oh, yes, you will."

"Give it a rest, Dex." Freddy sighed and opened her door. "Roll down your window to let in the breeze. I'll be back in no time."

Inside the front door of the Buckle Barn, she breathed in the new-leather scent and looked around for Ry.

Connie Davis, the owner and Duane's steady girl-friend for the past two years, rushed up to her and spoke in a conspiratorial whisper. "Is *he* the one from New York?" She tilted her head toward the back of the store. "The one you were so worried about?"

A giant cardboard cutout of Brooks and Dunn, a popular singing duo, blocked Freddy's view. "I guess. Tall guy, light brown hair, midthirties?"

"Beautiful blue eyes and shoulders that fill out a Western shirt?"

Freddy's breath hitched. She'd rather not think of Ry in those terms. "I suppose."

"You don't have a thing to worry about," Connie said.

"You're probably right. After tomorrow, he'll be back in New York and he can't very well dictate what goes on at the True Love from that distance."

"Going back?" Connie looked confused. "He told me he needed some clothes because he planned to be here at least another week."

Freddy's heart stilled momentarily. "Maybe you were talking to somebody else. Mr. McGuinnes made reservations at the ranch for three nights only."

"We can sure find out. Come on back. This fellow is making a final decision on a hat."

Freddy rounded the Brooks and Dunn display with Connie just as Ry pulled the brim of a black hat low over his eyes. He turned and gave her an easy smile. "Ready?"

She struggled to find a response. Outfitted in bor-rowed clothes, he'd looked pretty darn good, but noth-ing compared to the picture he made in jeans that hugged his thighs, supple cotton that moved with each shrug of his broad shoulders and a hat that shadowed his blue eyes, imbuing them with compelling mystery.

She wanted him out of town. "I thought you were leaving tomorrow," she said.

"Freddy!" Connie shot her a glance. "That wasn't very nice."

He regarded her steadily. "I've changed my mind."

"But your reservation—"

"You have available rooms. You said this was the slow season."

And the hot season, she thought, noticing how his chest hair peeked from the open neck of his shirt.

"Don't you need to get back? To Wall Street and everything?"

A corner of his mouth tilted up. "No, not as long as the phone lines work. Of course, I suppose you could go out with your wire cutters tonight and force that issue."

She gasped. "I would never do such a thing."

"Wouldn't you? You've resorted to just about everything else to get rid of me." He turned to pick up the rest of his clothes from a chair by the dressing room door. "But it isn't going to work, so you might as well get used to having me around."

9

AT ABOUT SIX-THIRTY that night, Freddy nudged Maureen into a trot as she and Ry rode along a trail near the southern boundary of the ranch. Freddy knew that Ry's mount, a dark bay named Destiny, would mimic her horse's pace, and she hoped the jouncing would knock some sense into Ry's thick skull. She wondered what he hoped to accomplish by staying on another week. Surely he recognized the volatile situation between them.

To their right, the sun sat like a bronze paperweight anchoring the horizon. Then, as if melting from its own heat, it gradually flattened and slipped out of sight. Above them the sky was clear except for a towering pile of white clouds that looked like a huge serving of vanilla ice cream. As the sun sank, the vanilla turned to strawberry, then raspberry, and finally orange sherbet.

It was Freddy's favorite time of day, when the heat had left the desert air yet there was still enough soft light for a rider to see the trail. A fierce love of this land surged within Freddy as she glanced over at Ry, the interloper. Did he imagine he could really own the True Love? Money wasn't enough to claim ownership.

"When does the real estate agent expect an answer on your offer?" she asked.

"Soon." Despite the trot, he sat on his horse easily, the reins held loosely in one hand, his denim-clad thighs gripping leather as he moved in rhythm with his mount. He pulled his hat brim lower to shade his eyes from the setting sun. "Duane asked me today about reinstating the rodeo."

"And what did you say?"

"I didn't give him a direct answer because I decided to settle it with you, first. We can't take risks like that with the guests, Freddy. No more rodeos."

So it starts, she thought. The greenhorn dictator. "You'll probably lose business," she said. "Lots of people come to the ranch just for the rodeo."

"I don't care. A lawsuit could bankrupt us."

Freddy sighed. That was big-city thinking, all right. And to be fair, he had a point. Her father had loved the rodeo and hadn't worried at all about lawsuits, but her father had been a lousy businessman. Maybe Ry and his partners would be the first to turn a profit from the True Love.

He paused and reined Destiny to the left. "Let's check out that herd of cattle over there."

Freddy surveyed the group of about twenty white-faced Herefords, their rusty coats burnished by the orange light of sunset. "That wouldn't be a good idea, Ry."

"Why not?"

Ordinarily, she'd have let him find out for himself, but all this talk about lawsuits had made her jittery. He didn't own the ranch yet, and she and Westridge would be responsible if he decided to sue. "Destiny's been trained as a cutting horse. Get him around a stray animal and he lays down some funky moves."

"Sounds like fun."

"Look, Ry, I don't think you understand. He—"

"Let me try, Freddy." He kicked Destiny into a lope. "How bad can it be?"

"Ry, slow down!" She started after him. "You'll spook them!" she called, too late to stop the cattle from scattering in several directions. They were used to crazy greenhorns, so they wouldn't run far, but any minute, she expected Destiny to spring into action.

He did.

Freddy groaned aloud, but still she loved watching the hairpin turns and dramatic spins of a good cutting horse working cattle. Ry seemed to love it less. First he lost his hat, then his stirrups. Finally, when Destiny sat back on his haunches and wheeled a hundred and eighty degrees after a bolting calf, Ry lost his seat and landed with a thud on the ground, catching part of a prickly pear on his way down. Destiny continued rounding up cattle with even more efficiency now that he'd dispensed with his bothersome rider.

Freddy started toward Ry. It wasn't as if she hadn't warned him, she thought. That should stand up in a courtroom. She leaned from the saddle and snatched his new hat from the branch of a creosote bush.

"Have you noticed that the cactus are in bloom?" she asked. "That beaver-tail prickly pear is especially pretty in yellow, don't you think?"

Ry looked up at her, his hair tousled, his face a grimace of pain.

She dismounted and dropped Maureen's reins to the ground before she walked toward him. One of the prickly pear pads had stuck to his left hip, but he'd avoided landing in the middle of the plant.

"Just think, you can tell all your friends you were thrown by one of the finest cutting horses in Arizona."

He rested his forearms on his bent knees. "I'm going to learn how to stay on that four-legged amusement ride," he said grimly.

"In a week? I don't imagine so. Leigh's a good teacher, but she can't work miracles." She crouched in front of him. "Here's your hat, and you seem to have a piece of prickly pear sticking to you."

His blue eyes met her gaze as he put on his hat. "I'm aware of that."

She didn't dare look into those eyes for very long. He might be a city slicker, but his calm acceptance of disaster was a very compelling trait, and there was no Dexter around to chaperon them this time. "You're lucky you didn't tangle with that cholla over there." She pointed to a jointed cactus with segments the size of hot dogs. "Now that's a cactus with an attitude."

"I'm developing one myself."

"Stay there and I'll help you get the cactus off." She pushed to her feet and looked around for a stick.

"What about my horse?"

She walked over to a dead palo verde. "Destiny will wander back once the cattle are rounded up. He's very well trained." She snapped off a dried branch and returned to where he sat. "Now hold still," she cautioned, crouching next to him again. "We might get all the needles to come out when I pry the cactus away."

"And if we don't?"

She studied the best point to slide the stick under the saucer-size paddle. "Unless you want to ride home this way, and drive the needles deeper, you'll have to take off your pants and hope they stay stuck in the denim."

"Shucking my pants is getting to be a habit around you."

"Trust me, it's not on purpose." She grasped his upper arm for balance as she maneuvered the stick gently between the thorns stuck into Ry's hip. His biceps tensed as the cactus moved, agitating the needles. "You can swear if you want," she offered.

"I appreciate that," he said through clenched teeth.

"I'll wedge the stick in just a little more, and then I'll try to knock off the cactus in one movement."

"Sounds peachy." He sucked in his breath. "You know, in New York, I'm a capable kind of guy. I can hail cabs and—*ouch*—choose good restaurants and anticipate a bull market better than most men. You'd be impressed."

"I'm impressed now." With a quick jerk, she separated the cactus from his jeans.

"God bless America, but that smarts!"

"I know." She studied the dirt-stained denim. "Hold still. There are a couple of thorns I can probably pull out with my fingers, and that may be it."

"Did you mean that?"

"Mean what?" Using her fingernails like tweezers, she gripped one of the two remaining barbs and pulled.

"Sh—sugar! About being impressed."

Had she said that? She'd been concentrating so hard on getting the cactus out of him, she must have spoken without thinking. Gradually, she became aware of her fingers closed securely over his arm, her face inches from his, their bodies hunched together. She glanced at him and found him studying her intently. Her breathing quickened. "One more thorn."

"You know, all along I've thought we couldn't become involved because we would be business associates."

"Exactly," she said, returning her attention to his hip and the last white needle that had pricked through the denim into his skin. She kept her gaze focused on that needle as she gripped it with her fingernails. She must not allow her gaze to wander to his thighs or worse, to the bulge between them. It was like telling herself not to look over the edge of a precipice. She couldn't resist, and a hollow ache began deep within her.

"But thanks to a comment from your sister, I started thinking about how different the rules are out here," he continued. "For instance, in New York, its manly to swear, even in front of women. But a true cowboy doesn't swear in front of women, does he?"

Even his voice, so close to her ear, was an aphrodisiac. Freddy prayed her trembling fingers would work well enough to pull out the last barb. "You're right. Most cowboys don't swear in front of women."

"And another thing I've noticed. In New York, everybody's scrambling for status and prestige. Out here, nobody wants to lord it over anybody. With the possible exception of Eb Whitlock."

"Oh, for heaven's sake. Eb's not so bad."

Ry made a dismissive sound deep in his throat. "He's probably the only person who would care if we were lovers."

She pulled too quickly and the needle broke off in the middle, leaving only a stub. "Rats!"

"Now what?"

There was one more thing she could do, and it was better than having him shed his pants right now, after that remark about becoming lovers. "I'll use my teeth."

He chuckled. "Oh, Freddy."

"Be quiet, Ry, before I lose my nerve."

"The day you lose your nerve, they'll have to send a national news team to cover it. What do you think of my theory?"

"I think it's dangerous." She took off her hat and laid it beside her.

"I want you, Freddy. And don't pretend you don't want me. It's too late for that."

"All I want is to get this last thorn out." Drawing a deep breath, she marked the spot with two fingers spread on either side of it. Then she leaned down and located the blunt needle with her tongue. The scent of denim, dust and potent male filled her nostrils. Warm rivers of desire coursed through her as she fastened her teeth on the end of the barb. With a twist of her head, she pulled it out and rose to a kneeling position beside him, the needle in her teeth.

"Here," he said softly, reaching to take it. His fingers brushed her mouth and his eyes darkened. He dropped the needle to the ground. She couldn't seem to move, couldn't summon even the faintest resistance as he cupped his hand behind her head and urged her closer.

"You want more than that, Freddy." His lips met hers in soft supplication. All the reasons that she shouldn't be doing this abandoned her with the first touch of those persuasive lips. The slightest feathering of his tongue gained him access to her mouth as she moaned in surrender. Cradling her head in both hands, he tasted her thoroughly. His kiss painted images of skin sliding against skin, of limbs entwined, of bodies thrusting as two become one.

Desire streaked through her like fire through dry brush. She'd chastised herself about responding so readily in the pool, but this was worse. She wanted him with a ferocity that urged her to pull him down to the dusty floor of the desert, rid herself of her restricting clothes and open her thighs to receive all he offered.

Breathing hard, he lifted his mouth from hers. She swayed, and he clasped her by the shoulders, holding her steady as much with his heated gaze as with the strength of his hands. "Open your blouse for me," he murmured.

She hesitated.

"Please, Freddy."

She unbuttoned the cotton shirt with quivering fingers and pulled it from the waistband of her jeans. When the blouse hung open, he stroked down the swell of her breasts and almost negligently flipped the front catch on her bra. Her breath caught as he parted the material, grazing her nipples with his palms.

His voice was husky. "I knew you'd look like this." He tossed his hat to the ground and captured her breasts in both hands. Closing her eyes, she arched upward, anticipating the hot moisture of his mouth. When it came, she sighed with satisfaction and tunneled her fingers through his hair.

Splaying his hand across her back, he held her steady for the onslaught of his lips and tongue and the gentle abrasion of his chin. Thought surrendered to sensation, logic to desire as she gave herself and delighted in the giving. Moistened with need, she begged softly for more.

"Not here," he whispered against her breast. Then, with a groan, he returned to her lips for a penetrating, mind-bending kiss.

A firm bump from the side nearly sent them both toppling over. Wrenched apart by the near fall, they turned in unison and confronted Destiny standing two feet from them, his flanks heaving.

"Go away," Ry said, waving his hand.

Destiny jerked his head up, but he remained where he was. Then he lowered his head and blew through his nostrils, spraying them.

"Ugh." Freddy wrinkled her nose and started mopping her breasts with the tail end of her shirt.

"Let me," Ry said, a trace of humor in his voice as he took the other end of her shirt and began a motion that was more caress than cleanup. "I thought you said he was well trained."

"That's exactly why he's standing there." She struggled to breathe normally, but Ry's touch made that difficult. "He's supposed to return to the spot where he left his rider."

"And blow snot on him?"

She smiled. "No, that's Destiny's specialty. I think he has springtime allergies."

"Remind me to buy him an antihistamine." Ry put his hands under her elbows and lifted her to her feet. "In the meantime, let's get out of the range of fire, go where we won't be so rudely interrupted."

She drew in a deep breath. Destiny had given her a second chance to be rational and she had to take it.

Ry gazed at her. "I see misgivings. Guess I'll have to kiss them away."

"No." She forced herself to step out of his embrace. "I think Destiny just saved us from making fools of ourselves." Avoiding his eyes, she refastened her bra and started in on the buttons of her shirt.

His frustration was evident as he put his hands on his hips and stared at the ground. He lifted his head. "I wouldn't have made love to you on top of a cactus, if that's what you were worried about."

She looked up at the soft gray of the sky, where Venus sparkled next to a sliver of moon. Tucking her shirt into her jeans, she turned and started back toward Maureen. "It's getting dark. We'd better go."

"Whoa, there, little filly." He caught her arm and turned her to face him again. "Back up for those of us who don't know the territory. A moment ago, you were begging me to love you, and now you're shutting me out. I'm entitled to an explanation. Are you worried about what people will think?"

"Not really. Around here, people mind their own business about things like that. No, the problem is with me."

He frowned.

"If it doesn't work out between us, the fallout could poison my whole existence at the ranch."

"It could also improve your existence at the ranch. Aren't you willing to take a chance that it might?"

She regarded him steadily. "No."

"My God but you're protective of the status quo!"

"You're right. I don't have your appetite for risk." She paused. "But that might be because I've found something worth hanging on to." She pulled from his grasp and walked to Maureen on unsteady legs. "We need to go. It's getting dark."

The dusk-to-dawn light had snapped on by the time Freddy and Ry reached the corral. Freddy noticed that Leigh was back from team-roping practice, and as they rode up, Leigh unloaded Pussywillow, one of her favorite mares, from the horse trailer. Freddy was glad for the company. The less time Freddy spent alone with Ry the better.

Leigh waved a greeting and turned the gray mare into the corral. Then she wandered over to the hitching post as Freddy and Ry dismounted. "Have a good ride?" she asked.

"Ry decided to test-drive Destiny through a herd of critters," Freddy said.

Leigh gave Ry a startled look. "You stayed on him?"

"No." Ry swung down and tipped his hat back as he talked to Leigh. "And I'd like to arrange a few riding lessons, so I'm ready for him next time."

As they discussed scheduling, Freddy pretended to be engrossed in unsaddling Maureen, but her attention remained on Ry. She was amazed at how much he looked like a cowboy now. He'd picked up the mannerisms, the walk, even the aggressiveness of cowboy lovers, she thought as heat rose to her cheeks. She hauled the saddle and blanket into the wing to the right of the barn, an old stone structure reserved for the tack used by the hands. Equipment for the dudes was segregated and kept in the newer tin wing on the opposite side of the barn.

As she started back out, Ry came through the door with Destiny's saddle and blanket. Duane had sponsored Ry's entry into the hands' tack room. She moved aside to let him pass and then started out of the shed as he settled his blanket and saddle on a wooden stand.

"Freddy."

She turned, and before she realized what he meant to do, he'd stepped forward and swept her into his arms. His lips came down quickly, stifling any possible protest, and in seconds he'd shattered her carefully built defenses.

Then he released her. "Think about that," he said. "I'm catching a ride up to the house with Leigh."

Long after he'd left the tack shed, Freddy stood in the same spot where he'd left her, fingers pressed to her love-sensitized mouth. Ry might be lacking riding skills, but his kiss needed no refinements whatsoever. She wanted him more than she'd ever wanted a man, almost more than she'd ever wanted anything...including the ranch.

10

ALL THE WAY BACK to the ranch house, Ry questioned Leigh about her team roping. The more he heard, the more he wanted to try it. Finally, he asked her if she'd teach him that, too.

"Let's improve your horsemanship first," she said with a dry chuckle. "You have to learn to walk before you can run."

"How long do you think it will take before I can start learning team roping?"

"Ambitious son-of-a-gun, aren't you?"

"Always have been, Leigh."

She nodded. "How are things going between you and my sister?"

Ry gazed out the window into the darkness. "She doesn't trust me."

"Should she?"

He couldn't answer that because he didn't know the answer himself. He wouldn't ever run out on a relationship, but that wasn't the issue with Freddy. She wanted a guarantee that she'd always be able to live on her ranch, and he couldn't promise her that. Life involved constant change. Invest too heavily in a certain future and you were bound to lose. He should know that more than anybody.

Leigh parked at the side of the house where Duane was still working on the other ranch vehicles. Ry thanked her for the ride and left her there conferring with Duane about the state of her truck's tires. A country line-dance lesson for the guests was in progress in the main room of the ranch house, the music and laughter spilling onto the wide front porch. A shadowy figure sat in a chair with another shadow at its feet. As Ry came closer, moonlight glinted off an aluminum walker next to the person in the cane chair.

Ry's boots clunked hollowly on the wooden porch as he crossed it—a nice sound, he thought. "Mind if I join you?" he asked Dexter.

"Nope."

The neighboring cane chair creaked as Ry sat down, and the black-and-white dog raised his head. Dexter didn't speak, just reached down and put a hand on the dog's head.

"Is he yours?" Ry asked.

"Yep. A mare. No, a girl."

"The dog's a female?"

"Yep."

"Oh. What's her name?"

"Don't know. Used to know."

Ry wondered what it would be like to have once been the foreman of this ranch, the person in charge of everything, and now be reduced to mail runs, trips for ice cream and lots of porch time. On top of that, it would be an exquisite kind of hell to understand everything going on around you, yet be unable to communicate much of anything without a struggle.

Dexter held up his left hand and pointed to his wedding ring. "Did you ever?"

"Get married?"

Dexter nodded.

Ry settled back in the chair as the lively beat of the music competed with the steady chirp of crickets. The mingled sounds felt cozy. He relaxed his head against the ladder-back of the chair. "Yes," he said. "I got married."

"Is it broken? I mean, no good?"

"She died."

"Too bad. When?"

"Eight years ago today. May 24."

Dexter was silent. Inside, the music ended, and someone laughed. The instructor said a few things, but Ry couldn't make out the words. Then the music began again.

"Five hundred—no—fifty. Fifty-two years," Dexter said at last.

Ry was beginning to get the hang of talking to Dexter and deciphering his cryptic messages. "That's a long time to be married."

"Yep."

"I envy you that."

"Yep."

Ry allowed himself a rare moment of nostalgic longing. He hadn't been raised to believe in roots and long-term relationships. His father's job had required moving his family many times, and when Ry was fifteen his parents had divorced. Ry and Linda had occupied at least five apartments in their brief marriage, and they'd agreed to postpone having children until they were "settled." Ry had always suspected they wanted to be sure they'd stay together before they took that drastic step.

He'd never had an attic or a basement stuffed with years of collected memories, never had an "old neighborhood" to go back to. He'd prided himself on being pared down, flexible, eager for challenge and change. A marriage that lasted for fifty-two years was almost beyond his comprehension. If he married today, he'd have to live to be eighty-seven to accomplish that. His thoughts drifted to Freddy, whose image was never far from his mind. She was the sort of woman who would expect her marriage to last fifty years.

"Dexter?" A woman came around the end of the house holding a glass in each hand. "Oh, is that you, Mr. McGuinnes?"

He stood. "Please call me Ry, Belinda."

She mounted the porch steps slowly but surely. "Would you like some iced tea?" she asked, holding out the glass.

He was pretty sure she'd intended one of the two iced teas for herself and that she'd expected to join Dexter on the porch. "Thanks, but I was about to go inside. It's been a long day."

"If you're sure," she said in her musical voice. "I wouldn't want to drive you away on such a lovely evening."

"Maybe tomorrow night I'll be more awake and I can enjoy this porch as it should be enjoyed." Sitting here with Freddy wouldn't be a bad way to spend an evening, he thought.

"Oh?" She paused in the act of handing Dexter his iced tea. "Doesn't your plane leave tomorrow?"

"I've decided to stay on a while longer."

"Good," Dexter said.

A pang of conscience assailed Ry as he said his goodnights and walked toward the front door. Dexter wouldn't be so friendly if he knew Ry's ultimate plans for the True Love. And Belinda wouldn't be offering him glasses of iced tea. Duane wouldn't have suggested bronc-riding lessons, and Leigh wouldn't have agreed to help him improve his horse-handling skills. As for Freddy, she would have seen him impaled on a giant cactus before she would have given herself to him as she had tonight. He felt like a fraud, and he didn't know what the hell to do about it.

THAT NIGHT, while going over some figures on the office computer, Freddy noticed that the calendar page for the day seemed to be missing. She hunted around, even checked the wastebasket, but it was definitely gone. It wasn't a big deal, except that it said something about the kind of person Ry was. She'd loaned him her office for the day, and apparently he'd made notes on her calendar. Then he'd torn off the page and taken it with him instead of writing his information on another sheet. It was either insensitive or secretive, and she didn't much care for either trait. She'd been right to repel his advances, she thought as she turned off the computer for the night.

FREDDY SPENT the next few days staying out of Ry's way. Strangely, considering his last kiss, he seemed to be avoiding her, too. Leigh worked with him first thing every morning, and he spent a good part of the day practicing what she'd taught him. During the brief glimpses Freddy had of him, she noticed how tanned his face had become and how his body, already lean, seemed tougher now.

On one hot, cloudless day that heralded the blistering summer to come, she rode out with Duane to check a break in the barbed wire that Duane thought looked deliberately cut. One of the cattle had become tangled in a loose end and had required considerable doctoring.

After assessing the damage, she had to agree with Duane that the wire had been cut.

"Don't you think you should tell Ry about all these things that have been happenin' 'round here?" Duane asked as they rode down the wide lane leading toward the corrals. "They're mostly piddly stuff, but they add up. I don't know if it's the jinx or some harebrained kids tryin' to be smart, but he should know he has a problem if the sale goes through."

"I'll tell him, but my credibility isn't too good these days. After all, I took him on that long trail ride just to get rid of him. Why wouldn't I make up a bunch of incidents to scare him away?"

Duane spat into the dirt. "Then I'll back you up."

"You were in on that trail ride thing. He probably won't believe you, either."

"Yes, he will, 'cause he knows I changed my mind about him. 'Course, we don't know what them partners of his are like, but he's okay. Having him own the True Love wouldn't be so bad. I think I can talk him into havin' a rodeo again."

"I don't think so, Duane. He told me he thought the liability was too great."

"He said that?" Duane scowled. "And here I went and strung up the barrel for him, too."

"You're teaching him to ride broncs? Talk about liability!"

"He wants to. Says he wants to try a bull, too."

"My God, that's insanity!"

"He asked me not to tell you, but I been feelin' bad about that, 'cause I figured you should know. And now I find out he don't want no rodeo. Maybe I jumped to conclusions about that greenhorn."

"Maybe we both did." She glanced at Duane. "What were you thinking of putting him up on, Grateful Dead?"

Duane shifted his chaw. "Come to think of it, I did mention that particular bull."

Her stomach twisted at the thought. "Duane, I'm sure you've been worried about this change of ownership, just like I have. So I have to ask. Was the bull riding just a way to make him hightail it back to New York?"

Duane shook his head vigorously. "No, ma'am. I swear that wasn't my idea originally. But now that I know he's against the rodeo, it's a thought, ain't it?"

"Absolutely not! The ranch doesn't belong to him yet. He could still sue both me and Westridge." Freddy told herself that was her chief concern. But a picture of Ry beneath the furious hooves of Grateful Dead kept spoiling her calm objectivity. A few riding lessons and a few turns on the bouncing barrel didn't make somebody a rodeo cowboy, but Ry didn't realize that.

She heard the whooping and hollering before she and Duane rounded the bend leading to the corrals. "What the—?" She urged Maureen into a faster trot around the curve. Ahead of her, the hands sat on the top rail of the main corral cheering a wildly bucking bay and its determined rider. Her blood ran cold as she saw who was on board.

"Oh, Lordy, he's on Gutbuster," Duane said.

"Not for long." Freddy leaped from her horse and threw the reins to Duane. "Hold Maureen," she called as she ran toward the corral. She made it just as Gutbuster spun and showed his belly in his famous "sunfish" move. Ry rose in a graceful arc and came down with a sickening thud that plowed his shoulder into the trampled dirt.

Freddy climbed the fence and shoved one of the hands aside as she jumped into the corral. "Somebody get that damned horse!" she cried as she ran toward Ry.

He lay completely still on his side, his back to her. His cherished black hat rested brim-side up nearby. Fear closed her windpipe. Dropping to her knees, she pressed two fingers against his neck just as he rolled over, bumping into her knees.

"And I thought you didn't care," he said with a wicked grin.

She jerked her hand away. "What in hell do you think you were doing?"

He pushed himself to a sitting position and started brushing the dirt from his shoulder. "Celebrating. And why are you swearing? I thought that wasn't allowed in the Code of the West?"

Anger shot through her, replacing her bone-deep fear. She jumped to her feet. "I should have you horse-whipped! You deliberately waited until Duane was with me and Leigh was out on a trail ride with the guests, didn't you? Of all the stupid, irresponsible, insane—" She paused, remembering something he'd said. "Celebrating what?"

He stood and gazed at her, his blue eyes sparkling. "Our offer was accepted this morning. The closing's in two weeks. You're looking at the new owner of the True Love Guest Ranch."

"I'm looking at an idiot! The sale's not final yet, and until it is, I'm still the foreman around here. You are *not* to ride one of our broncs again. There's no telling what could happen to you. Although I doubt that anything could crack that hard skull of yours, people have been known to die *coming* off a bronc." To her dismay, she realized the last sentence came out almost a sob.

He leaned down, picked up his hat and whacked it against his thigh to knock off the dust. "If I didn't know better, I'd think you were sweet on me," he said. Then he put on his hat, adjusted the brim and walked away.

Duane hurried up trailing a litany of apologies. "I shouldn't have fixed him up with that barrel, Freddy. I can see that now. I never dreamed he'd talk one of the boys into saddlin' Gutbuster. Guess I should have knowed it would happen, though. He's the kind that likes provin' himself, but I won't teach him no more. I won't—"

"Never mind, Duane." Freddy gazed after Ry as he walked to the opposite end of the corral and climbed the fence. On the other side stood several of the hands waiting to congratulate him. Covered with dust and looking proud as a peacock, he couldn't be distinguished from the other cowboys who were shaking his hand and clapping him on the back.

"They say he made the eight seconds," Duane said. "Curtis had a stopwatch on him. I wonder if he'll change his mind 'bout the rodeo now."

Freddy barely registered the information. She was too busy assimilating her feelings. When she'd seen him lying so still in the middle of the corral, she'd felt as if someone had ripped out her heart. And until the moment he rolled over, she'd sent a stream of prayers heavenward on his behalf. As foreman of the ranch, she had reason to be upset when someone took foolish chances, but she'd been more than upset. She'd been frantic.

"You won't want to hear this, but I've seen a lot of rodeo cowboys," Duane said. "There's a rhythm to it you can't teach. He's got it. Born with it, probably."

She swallowed the lump of emotion in her throat. "But he's a commodities trader," she murmured, resisting with all her might the urge to run across the corral, wrap her arms around him and beg him not to take such reckless chances.

"Not today he wasn't. Today he was a cowboy who rode a bronc to the buzzer."

THE NEXT MORNING, the ranch van hauled nine German tourists to the True Love, and that afternoon another twelve arrived. Because German groups had spent time at the ranch before, Freddy had picked up enough of the language to get by. So she was able to interpret the complaint when one of the couples said they'd been expecting to sleep in the John Wayne Room. They'd traveled halfway around the world to sleep there, they insisted.

Freddy stood with them in the large living room and tried to explain that they were lucky to get the honeymoon cottage, which was bigger, had a better view and more privacy. The couple shook their heads and began demanding the room they'd dreamed about "for many months."

Ry walked in just as Freddy was starting her fourth polite explanation of why the room was unavailable. He paused to listen and finally sauntered over to the group. Then, in perfect German, he offered to exchange sleeping accommodations with the couple.

The woman practically threw herself into Ry's arms, and the husband beamed and pumped Ry's hand enthusiastically. They chattered so fast in German that Freddy lost most of the conversation, but she would have had trouble following a conversation in English with Ry standing so close and looking so virile, his thumbs hooked through the loops in his jeans. Washing had shrunk them to a delicious fit that defined his shape beautifully. His boots and hat had seen more wear in a week than most cowboys gave them in a month, giving him a rugged aspect that could only be bought with experience on a cattle ranch.

One look into his laughing eyes as he talked with the Germans and she remembered those eyes darkening with passion, those lips capturing hers, those long tanned fingers caressing her. Yet after that last impassioned kiss, he'd made no move in her direction. Was he clever enough to realize that by backing away, he'd make himself even more appealing? Perhaps. Standing next to him now, she had to exercise self-control to keep from laying her hand on his arm, just to see if he'd react.

Partly to distract herself, she snagged a passing maid and gave the woman instructions to move Mr. Mc-Guinnes's belongings to the cottage and prepare the John Wayne Room for new guests. By the time she turned back, the couple was gone.

"Where are they?" she asked Ry.

"I suggested they order a cool drink and sit out by the pool while their room is cleaned. Otherwise, I figured they'd monopolize your time until the maid makes the switch, and you look like you have your hands full."

"Thanks. I do." *With you.* "What were they saying? My German's not that good."

He laughed. "They said I don't look like a guest."

"They're right. You don't. And what were they saying about John Wayne? I thought I heard something about a spirit. Don't tell me they're into seances, or something."

"No. They said I could be a reincarnation of John Wayne, I guess because I'm tall and I'm wearing Western clothes."

"And speaking German. They've probably seen dubbed versions of his movies. It must have been a fantasy come true to stand here talking to a real live cowboy who speaks German."

"You think I'm a real live cowboy?"

She didn't dare tell him her exact thoughts, that he was the best-looking stud in the valley. "Let's just say a tourist would think you were. Where did you learn German?"

"I picked up most of it on business trips."

She was beginning to get a picture of the astounding reach of Ry McGuinnes. "Then I assume you know some other languages?"

"*Oui, ma chérie.*" His gaze probed hers, seducing her as his mouth curved into a slow, sexy smile.

She was losing her composure fast in the spell cast by those suggestive eyes. There were reasons that she hadn't thought it wise to become his lover, but she couldn't think of a single one at the moment. Then she remembered the calendar page he'd apparently destroyed. "Did you rip a page out of my desk calendar the other day?" she asked abruptly.

The sensuality faded from his expression. "Yes, I did. Crumpled it up, too, so I didn't think you'd want it back."

"Are you in the habit of doing that with other people's possessions?" she pressed, relieved to have found something to dispel the passion that had begun to materialize between them.

His expression hardened. "No, I'm not. I still have it. Maybe I can iron it out for you, if it's so important. Now, if you'll excuse me, I have to get down to the corral and lay claim to Red Devil before Leigh changes her mind about letting me ride him."

"Red Devil?" She was now fully ready to be perverse. "I'd choose a different horse if I were you. He's thrown two of the hands already. The surgery didn't calm him down much."

His eyes narrowed. "Are you worried about the horse or the rider?"

"Neither, come to think of it," she retorted. "You probably deserve each other. Personally, I don't like riding a horse that gives me a fight."

His teeth flashed white in his tanned face and his eyes gleamed with a wicked fire. "But that's the fun of it, *Liebchen.*"

11

RED DEVIL TRIED a little crow-hopping and tossing of his head, but Ry felt in control as he walked the big chestnut horse away from the corrals. Leigh had told him Red Devil had been "cut proud," the cowboy way of describing a gelding who acted like a stallion. Ry liked that. Once the ranch deal went through, he'd own a third of Red Devil, but he'd decided to buy out Chase's and Joe's shares of the horse.

He hadn't made the decision lightly. The commodities market had taken some strange turns in the past few days, and he'd had to scramble to protect his assets. Just before he'd walked out of his room and discovered Freddy embroiled with the German couple, he'd completed a telephone call getting him into the corn market and out of soybeans, both in the nick of time. He'd burned the midnight oil figuring ways to hedge his bets on the gold and silver market so he'd wouldn't have any trouble coming up with his share of the ranch down payment. And through all that, he'd continued to take part in ranch life.

It was a test, to see if he could manage his investments from Arizona. If he could do it without suffering significant losses, he'd be able to spend more time on the True Love, more time riding Red Devil, more time polishing his bronc-riding skills. And more time with Freddy. She was resisting him, perhaps from some instinctive sense that he represented change in her life. He wanted to find a way to make her welcome that change, because, try as he might to put her out of his mind, he wanted Freddy.

Just then, a white sedan came down the road toward him, driving fast and sending up a rooster tail of dust. Ry frowned and got a firmer grip on Red Devil's reins. Damned city people. Then he smiled at himself. He was acclimating fast.

The car slowed as it came alongside Red Devil. The horse pranced sideways and arched his neck. Ry reined him in and gripped with his thighs. "Easy, Red. Easy," he murmured.

The tinted window of the sedan buzzed down and a man in suit and tie stuck his head out. The car's air-conditioning wafted around Ry and he found himself thinking the guy was a wimp to need air-conditioning. It couldn't be much over ninety.

The man took off his sunglasses and squinted up at Ry. "Say, cowboy, am I headed in the right direction for the True Love Guest Ranch?"

Being addressed as a cowboy made Ry's day, even though the man's attitude wasn't particularly respectful. "Straight ahead and take a right at the fork," he said, tightening the reins as Red Devil pranced some more.

"That's quite a horse you have," the man said.

"Yep." Ry almost wished he chewed tobacco so he could spit in the dirt after that reply.

"Thanks for the directions." The automatic window buzzed upward and the car took off, spewing fumes and leaving a billowing cloud of dust to settle over Ry and Red Devil.

Cursing and wiping grit from his face, Ry loped away from the dust and exhaust fumes. Only later, as he traversed the now-familiar western end of the True Love, did he figure out who the guy might be. An environmental engineer was due out any time, to check the water and make sure nothing toxic was buried under the True Love. Ry longed for the necessary paperwork to be finished. Chase had mentioned during his last phone call that he might make it out in time for the closing. It wasn't necessary—everything could be handled by mail—but Ry could understand Chase's eagerness to be part of the process. Besides, without a rig to drive someplace, the trucker seemed to be getting very bored.

Ry thought of the impact the ranch would have on a hot-blooded young rebel like Chase and laughed. If the Gutbuster incident got Freddy's undies in a bunch, wait till she tried to control Lavette.

THE COUPLE WHO'D wanted the John Wayne Room wasn't Freddy's only problem that afternoon. The environmental engineer arrived and she had to provide him with a map of the buildings and outbuildings. Then several of the German guests announced they were vegetarians, precipitating a conference with Belinda on the menu, which was ordinarily built around beef. A young woman started sneezing and insisted her room be cleaned again with damp cloths to pick up all the dust. Freddy suggested allergy medicine, but the woman claimed she never took pills.

"So she comes to a guest ranch in the desert in May," Freddy mumbled to herself as she located Rosa, the housekeeper, and requested the second cleaning.

She'd just ducked into her office to call the bunkhouse and ask for six horses to be saddled for a sunset ride, when Dexter appeared in the doorway leaning on his walker, his best hat sitting jauntily on his head. "Hi, Dex," she said, picking up the phone and punching in the bunkhouse extension. "What can I do for you?"

"Ice cream."

She'd forgotten. She glanced quickly at her calendar and sure enough, today was ice-cream day. One look into Dexter's face alight with expectation and she ditched the idea of putting off the ice-cream trip until the next day. "Sure," she said. "Right after this call."

"Okay." He pivoted his walker and stumped toward the double doors leading to the porch.

In ten minutes, she'd arranged for the sunset ride and had asked Leigh to handle any problems with the guests or the environmental engineer. As Freddy pulled the van up to the arched entryway, Dexter had barely made it down the flagstone path. She guided him in with as little fuss as possible, knowing he hated needing the help. But these days, his ice-cream trip was more important than his vanity.

As they headed toward the main road, a lone rider stood on a rise about a mile to their left. Even from that distance, Freddy recognized Ry on Red Devil. Red Devil tossed his head but otherwise stood quietly. Ry seemed to have perfect control of the big animal, she thought with a pang of resentment. Why should this greenhorn be able to master a horse when some of her experienced hands had failed? Yet Ry sat like a king in the saddle as he gazed out over the land.

Freddy returned her attention to the road, but the picture of Ry surveying the ranch stayed with her. Her father used to do that, and so had she, on occasion. She remembered the possessive feeling of those moments, and she grew uneasy. The True Love belonged to the Singleton family, no matter who held the deed. At least, that's the way it had always been.

Dexter craned his head backward, still looking at Ry silhouetted on the promontory. "His mother—no—his girl died," Dexter said.

"His wife died," Freddy said. "I know. He told me."

"May 24."

Freddy felt as if someone had dropped ice cubes in her stomach. That was the date on the missing calendar page. But maybe Dexter's comments weren't related to each other. "What about May 24?" she asked.

"She died."

Freddy swallowed. "How do you know that, Dexter?"

"He said."

"He told you his wife died on May 24?"

"Yep."

SOMEHOW Freddy made it through the rest of her duties that day. Ry ate in the dining room, but he'd been appropriated by the couple now sleeping in the John Wayne Room, and Freddy spent most of the meal counseling the young woman with the allergies about not going outside during the early morning and late afternoon, when the pollen count was highest.

Then the sunset-ride crowd came in, and Freddy got caught up in their stories of seeing a pack of coyotes chasing down a rabbit. Some of the riders seemed to think Freddy should do something about protecting the cute little bunnies, so she spent another hour convincing them that they were looking at real nature, not something created as a theme park.

It was almost nine before she broke free. She looked around for Ry, but he was gone. She checked the porch, even asked the couple who had spent most of the evening with him, but nobody could tell her where he was. At last, she decided to try the cottage.

The John Wayne Room couple had blown it, she thought as she approached the small building, which was a miniature of the main house, complete with red-tiled roof, whitewashed adobe and a front porch shaded with a sweet-smelling jasmine vine. Freddy always gave the cottage to honeymooning couples, but none had presented themselves in the German group, so she'd picked at random, thinking she'd offered them a treat.

Ry wasn't sitting on one of the Adirondack chairs occupying the front porch, but a light shone from the window. Freddy tapped on the door.

"Come in," he called, and she opened the carved door, wondering why he hadn't bothered to get up to answer the knock.

He was sitting on the bed talking on the phone, his briefcase open beside him and papers spread over the white comforter. He glanced up, his eyes widening. He covered the mouthpiece. "I'll just be a minute."

She half turned toward the door. "I could come back—"

"No. I'll be through soon."

She pulled out one of the captain's chairs next to a small table in the corner and sat down. She hadn't been in here for a while and had forgotten the charm of the decor. She automatically checked for cobwebs in the beamed ceiling or any yellowing of the Battenburg lace trimming the white comforter and the curtains at the windows. Like most of the beds at the ranch, the one in the cottage was an antique four-poster paired with a dark wood dresser and end table. Ry's hat hung on a post at the foot of the bed, in typical cowboy fashion. His boots were propped in a corner, and his shirt was unsnapped almost to his waist. It was warm in the room, and Freddy wondered if the air conditioner was broken. She'd have to ask.

Everything else looked in good shape. From what she could see of the bathroom, the clawfoot tub looked clean and the towels neatly arranged. The bathroom's tile floor gleamed in the light from the bedroom, and the pine floors of the bedroom looked recently oiled. No stains marred the geometric-patterned Indian rugs on the floors. As Freddy might have expected, Rosa ran a tight ship. Everything was perfect.

"No, I want to get into Eurodollars now," Ry said, running his fingers through his hair. "I know that's risky but I think it'll pay off. I appreciate your handling this for me." He paused and looked over at Freddy. "It's great. Riding bucking broncos and everything." He winked at Freddy. "You bet! Bring Susie and the kids. Okay. Talk to you tomorrow."

He hung up the phone and started gathering up the papers. "To what do I owe this honor?"

Freddy's grip tightened on the arm of the chair. She'd been practicing her apology ever since Dexter had dropped his bombshell. But now words deserted her. She didn't know where to begin. "Isn't your air conditioner working?" she asked instead.

"It's working." He tapped the papers together and tucked them into his briefcase. "I'm just getting used to the heat, I guess. I decided not to turn it on." He snapped the case closed and put it beside the bed.

"So I see."

He glanced down at his unbuttoned shirt. "Does this offend you, ma'am?" he asked with a deadpan expression.

No, it excited her. She took refuge in a bored tone of voice. "Of course not. I work around a ranch full of men who sometimes, believe it or not, take off their shirts in my presence."

"Funny, but my experience around you has had more to do with pants than shirts."

She flushed, or maybe it was just the heat affecting her. But if he could live without air-conditioning, so could she. After all, she was the one raised in this country; he'd been here less than two weeks. "I didn't mean to interrupt your work," she said, gesturing toward the briefcase. "It must be difficult keeping up with Wall Street when you're this far away."

"It's been difficult, but possible, which is something I wanted to find out. I'll definitely need to spend time in New York, but not as much as I thought at first."

She stared at him. "You sound as if you're planning to take up residence at the True Love."

His gaze was steady. "I am."

"Why?"

"Because I like it here."

She hadn't counted on this. Not by a long shot. "You'd uproot yourself just like that? Change your whole life?"

"I think you advised me once to get a life."

"I was joking. Surely you have ties to New York, people you don't want to leave."

He nodded. "Two couples Linda and I spent time with, and a good friend who works in commodities with me. I just talked to him. You heard me invite him and his family out here, and I'll go back there from time to time. It's not as if I have to spend weeks on a stagecoach to keep in touch."

"But life out here is so *different*."

"Which is why I like it. I've discovered I'd rather ride Red Devil than play handball with the guys at the gym."

She swallowed the nervousness rising in her throat. "What about . . . girlfriends?"

"Why do you want to know?" he asked with a smile.

Heat rose to her cheeks. "Never mind. I don't want to know."

"Yes, you do. I've dated in the past few years, but nothing's ever clicked. In other words, I don't have a lover waiting for me back home, Freddy." The warmth of his gaze made her look away in confusion.

"We have a limited number of guest rooms," she said, studying the pattern of the Indian rug. "I'm not sure where you will be able to stay. We already have several weekends booked solid for the winter season."

Ry appeared unfazed by her objection. "Then I'll sleep in the bunkhouse. I noticed not every bed is in use down there. If necessary, I'll set up a cot in the tack shed. Don't worry. I won't take up much space."

"The bunkhouse?" She glanced up. "That doesn't seem like the right place for one of the owners."

"Don't worry about it. Besides, I can't very well make you or Leigh sleep there, although the hands would think it was a fine idea. According to Duane, most of them get up every morning with a song of happiness on their lips because they work for those good-looking Singleton sisters."

Freddy examined a worn spot on the knee of her jeans. "Duane talks too much."

"He talks a lot more than I would have given him credit for when he picked me up at the airport. I guess he really hates big cities."

Freddy chuckled and looked up. "He sure does. He says if we ever give him his walking papers, we might as well shoot him and get it over with. He needs to stay near Tucson because his ex-wife and two kids are here, and there aren't a lot of ranching jobs in the area, so he'd be stuck looking for a job in town. Can you imagine Duane flipping burgers?"

"No." He paused. "Duane's not too happy with me at the moment. I guess you told him I wasn't in favor of reinstating the rodeo."

"I didn't think it was a secret."

"It isn't." A corner of his mouth turned up. "But now he's threatening to put my saddle in the greenhorn tack shed."

"I'm not surprised. There are two people you don't want to get on the wrong side of around here. Duane's one, and Belinda's the other."

"Belinda?" He raised his eyebrows. "She's the sweetest lady I've ever met."

"Cross her and see how sweet she is. She'd do anything to protect those near and dear to her. So would Duane, for that matter."

"Then it looks as if I'd better find a way to pacify Duane."

"By having a rodeo?" she asked.

"No."

"But you love riding broncs!"

"And I can't very well sue myself, can I?"

Freddy knew she was stalling, putting off the moment she'd have to apologize for making an issue of the calendar page. Facing this subject was much tougher than rising with dignity out of the horse trough. She looked down at her hands and laced her fingers together as she tried to remember how she'd planned to word her statement.

"What is it, Freddy?"

Startled by the nearness of his voice, she lifted her head and discovered he'd left the bed and crossed the room to stand in front of her. "I owe you an apology," she said softly.

"What for now?"

She frowned. "That wasn't nice."

"Sometimes I'm not nice." His eyes had darkened to navy as he stood before her in his bare feet, his shirt open just enough for her to follow the downward spiral of his chest hair to the waistband of his jeans. The scent of horse, male sweat and musk assailed her.

"I didn't realize when I made such a thing of that calendar page that you . . . that it was the day when . . . Ry, I didn't know. Dexter told me. If I'd only realized . . ." She trailed off, failing miserably to make the smooth statement of regret she'd practiced so many times in her head.

"I know," he said gently. "And I wasn't man enough to tell you the reason I ripped it out. It's not your fault."

She swallowed and looked away. He was man enough for anything she could imagine.

"Was that why you came here?"

She nodded. "I felt terrible. You must still love her very much."

He gazed out the window and shoved his hands in his pockets. "I'll always care about her, but that isn't why I mangled your calendar page," he said at last.

Freddy sat very still. She sensed the slightest movement or word from her might send him back behind the wall he'd built around this tragedy.

When he spoke, his voice was a strained monotone. "Even after eight years, I hate being reminded of that day because I keep thinking I should have been able to do something to keep it from happening." He looked at her, his expression tormented. "Punks, that's all they were!

Not one of them with a tenth of her potential. When she wouldn't give them her briefcase, which was typical of Linda's defiant attitude, they shot her." He snapped his fingers. "Gone, like that, all that talent, beauty, sense of humor." He began to pace the length of the room. "When the cops finally got them, they couldn't understand the big deal! They had no idea what they'd done with that one, impersonal bullet." His voice dropped to a whisper. "No idea."

Freddy got to her feet, her heart beating a slow, painful rhythm. No one should have to endure something like this, she thought. And certainly not alone. "It was random violence," she murmured, crossing to him and resting her hands lightly on his arms. "You couldn't have stopped it."

He met her gaze. "Maybe not. But when we were first married, I'd meet her at her office and we'd walk home together. Then our schedules got crazy and I stopped doing it. If I'd kept it up, then—"

"She would have accused you of overprotecting her," Freddy said, tightening her grip on his arms.

The anguish in his eyes eased a fraction and he nodded. "Probably."

"I would have," she continued. "I'd never stand for some man chaperoning me everywhere, implying I couldn't take care of myself."

His hands came up to cup her elbows and he smiled faintly. "I know. You remind me of her sometimes."

Freddy relaxed her grip and stepped back. Was that what this was all about? She didn't want to be a reminder of his late wife.

"And you didn't appreciate my saying that, did you?"

She crossed her arms in front of her chest. "I guess no woman wants to be a stand-in."

With a short humorless laugh, he reached for her, grabbing her arms and pulling her resistant body close enough that his breath feathered against her face. "That's the last thing I'd ever label you, Frederica Singleton. You're unique, and you've been driving me crazy since the day I saw you."

She lifted her chin. "Because I'm like Linda?"

"I'm attracted to strong women. You fit in that category, and so did Linda, but that's where it ends, Freddy." His voice grew tender as a caress. "When we kiss, it's you I'm kissing." His fingers kneaded the pliant flesh of her upper arm. "When I ache for a lover, you're the one I want." His words became a whisper. "You, Freddy."

Her pulse raced as she gazed into the flame-bright depths of his eyes. The heat pouring from him liquefied the brittle shell that had surrounded her for so long, she'd almost forgotton what it was like to be drenched in desire, to feel the surge of that warm river swelling against the moist confinement of its banks, threatening to overflow.

"And now I'll ask you again," he murmured. "Is your apology the only reason you came here tonight?"

12

"No," Freddy said. Ry's question opened a new freshet of passion within her. "No. I wanted to see you. Be with you."

"Ready to risk a little?"

"Maybe."

His gaze smoldered. "We don't have any excuses this time. There's nothing wrong with me. I don't need doctoring because I'm saddle-sore or full of cactus. You're dealing with a completely healthy male animal, no handicaps to slow me down."

Heart pounding, she deliberately moistened her lips. "Then if you don't need doctoring . . . what do you need, cowboy?"

His reply was husky. "I thought you'd never ask."

If he hadn't held her steady, she might have crumpled like a rag doll when his demanding lips found hers. But she needed his mouth against hers, needed it with a ferocity that made her wind both arms around his neck and hang on, moaning at the sweet invasion of his tongue. The heat of the room seemed fitting, matching the heat inside her, calling forth moisture that slicked her skin, readied it for love.

He snapped open the clip holding her hair and dropped it to the table beside them. Then, as he kissed her into oblivion, he combed her hair with his fingers, starting at her scalp and stroking downward. It was one of the most sensuous feelings she'd ever known, being kissed while he caressed her hair.

Slowly he released her and guided her back to the chair, where he got to one knee and pulled off one of her boots. Then, holding her gaze, he tugged off the other. Her breathing grew shallow.

"We'll have to be inventive," he said. "I'm not... prepared for this wonderful gift you've given me."

"Oh!" And she, a grown woman, wasn't, either. Embarrassment crept up her cheeks. "Then maybe we shouldn't—"

"Yes, we should. Within boundaries."

"Ry, I think I should go."

"No you don't." Taking her by the elbows, he brought her upright and pulled her close. "Only a man with no imagination would let you go out that door tonight."

"But—"

"I'm not that man." Cradling her bottom in both hands, he picked her up. Despite her misgivings, she wrapped her legs around him, tightening the contact. His manhood, held captive in snug denim, swelled in response.

"Ry, this is crazy. We should—"

"Quiet, madam foreman." He sat on the edge of the bed, holding her firmly in his lap, keeping her pressed tight against him. He kissed the corners of her mouth, her chin, the base of her throat, detonating land mines of sensation everywhere he touched. "From the first day, when I rode behind you and watched your tempting backside posting up and down in the saddle, I've dreamed of touching you like this, and I'm not waiting. I know what I'm doing."

She couldn't argue that one as he popped open the first snap of her shirt and eased her back just enough to flick his tongue against the widening vee he'd created. With a sigh, she bared her throat in surrender.

"And then you massaged ointment on my thighs," he murmured as snaps gave way to his questing fingers. "Do you have any idea the image you created, bending over my lap like that?"

"I didn't want you . . . to be in pain." She was having a hard time thinking as he reached for the front clasp of her bra and her breasts began to ache in anticipation.

"There are many kinds of pain, *ma chérie*."

"Some can be . . . sweet."

"If you know that someone will soon relieve it." He lowered his head and took her nipple between his teeth, biting gently. She moaned.

He cradled her breast and licked the heated surface. "You're so cool-looking on the outside, but on the inside—" he nibbled at the turgid peak once more "—you're so hot, you could burn a man."

Desire roughened her voice. "Are you afraid?"

"No." He lifted his head to look into her eyes. "I love the fire." He unhooked her belt and pulled it through the loops. "I love to build it and I love to see it burn."

Through eyes heavy-lidded with passion, she met the challenge in his gaze. Astraddle him like this, she was already open to him, completely vulnerable to his plans, save for some insignificant layers of material. He unfastened her jeans and pulled the zipper down. They were old jeans, soft and pliable from long wear. They easily accommodated the hand that Ry slipped inside the opening. Unerringly, he found her sensitive spot with the heel of his hand and pressed against the damp cotton of her underwear.

She caught her lower lip between her teeth, holding back a small cry.

"Oh, no," he said. "We'll have none of that. Not in this secluded little cottage. Not when the guests are all inside with their air conditioners running." He rotated the heel of his hand against her with lazy precision that wound the spring ever tighter. "I want it all, Freddy. Lose it for me. Let me see the tigress in heat."

She closed her eyes and whimpered.

"That's better." A breath later, he'd pushed aside the cotton barrier and slipped his fingers deep inside her. "Now let's turn up the flame."

She moaned as he initiated an insistent rhythm.

"Yes." His breathing quickened. "More, Freddy." He rubbed her tight knot of desire with his thumb. "Give me more."

She didn't recognize the small cries of need he wrung from her. It was as if she had no choice but to moan and sigh as his clever fingers probed pressure points she'd never guessed existed. The flames licked around her, through her. She gripped his shoulders as the only anchor in a whirling maelstrom where she wondered if pleasure had the power to make her fly apart into a million pieces. She sensed the moment coming, almost heard it like the rumble of a distant waterfall, and then she was pitched headlong past all restraint, flung gasping into the convulsing world of release.

As she shuddered in his arms, he kissed her back to sanity, cupping her face and stroking her hair away from her damp forehead. "You are so beautiful," he said. "I thought so before, but now that I've seen you like this..."

Dazed, she laid her head on his shoulder. "Oh, Ry."

He cuddled her, holding her like a precious artifact. "I knew there was that kind of passion in you."

"I didn't," she murmured.

"You didn't?" The male satisfaction in his voice made her smile.

She lifted her head so he could see that smile. "You wanted me to lose it. I sure did."

"I wanted just what I got, you in a frenzy, so wet and flushed, so willing for me to..." He trailed off and sucked in his breath.

The desire in his eyes told her most of what she needed to know, and a quick glance downward supplied confirmation. He needed her, and she wanted to give. Ry wasn't the only one who'd had fantasies.

She began slowly, reaching inside the open front of his shirt to find his nipples buried in a swirl of chest hair. She scratched across the tips lightly with her fingernails and was rewarded with another sharp intake of breath.

She gazed into his eyes. "I think you might need doctoring, after all."

The look he gave her was hot enough to start a fire in wet kindling. "Could be."

Her shirt was damp. She flicked open the snaps at her wrists. "Let me slip into something more comfortable." With a shrug of her shoulders, the shirt slipped to the floor. She flung her bra after it. "There." When she glanced at Ry to gauge the effect, she was rewarded by the flash of primitive lust in his gaze.

Still astride him, she rose to her knees, her hands cupping her breasts. "See anything you like, cowboy?"

With a groan, he pulled her close, tasting, nipping, suckling. She'd thought to tease him, to drive him a little crazy before she gave him relief, but his teeth tugging at her nipples renewed the fire deep in her loins, and she began to quiver with her own need. She pulled away, breathing hard, and applied herself to the task of unfastening his belt. He pulled her back, toppling them both to the bed as he ravished her breasts.

Before she realized it, he'd nudged her out of her already unfastened jeans and stripped away her panties. Free of restriction, she wanted him in a way that threatened to destroy all reason. Had she imagined she could control a conflagration this powerful?

No longer caring about anything but bringing him inside her, she opened the fly of his jeans and reached beneath the elastic of his briefs. Stroking the fullness there, she begged him to love her. Now.

Gasping, he looked into her eyes. "You tempt me, wicked woman."

"Love me, Ry. Please love me."

He took a long, shuddering breath. "Fantasies first. That time, when you were putting on the ointment, you gave me a picture that won't go away. Give me the reality."

Of course she would. She would do anything for him, despite the aching, driving passion clamoring for his attention.

He lifted his hips and she divested him of his clothes. He was magnificently, achingly aroused. Her fingers closed over the hot shaft. She leaned down, knowing he was watching her. Her tongue tasted salty desire, and the need to love him overrode her need to be loved. His groan as she enclosed him made the sacrifice of her own satisfaction pale to nothing.

He shifted position, but she was so involved in his pleasure that she didn't realize his purpose until he touched the burgeoning point of her own excitement and a spasm of pleasure zinged through her. Then his mouth was there, loving her with a thoroughness that made her dizzy. Somehow, despite the exquisite distraction, she ministered to him, too. His moment came first, and she rejoiced in the great shudders that shook his body. Soon after, he lavished her with an equal gift that left them sated and panting.

He eased up beside her and pulled her close. Silently, they held each other, knowing words could add nothing to such unabashed sharing of pleasure. They breathed in unison, as if they'd synchronized all their responses.

"Stay the night," he murmured at last.

"Isn't that dangerous? We might forget and—"

"If I didn't forget that time, when I could hardly see from wanting you, I won't forget. Stay."

"I'll stay." She snuggled closer.

"But don't expect to sleep much," he murmured, his voice husky in her ear.

"We only have about seven hours until dawn. Will that be enough time for what you have in mind?"

"No. But I can't do everything I have in mind. Tomorrow, we'll pick up what we need to expand our horizons, and we can take it from there."

A delicious tightening in her groin was followed by a realization that it might not be so easy to buy the supplies he was referring to. "We can't get them in La Osa," she said.

"Tucson, then. Because tomorrow night, I intend—"

"I'm sure you do," she said, laying a finger over his lips. "I'll buy some in Tucson. I'll find some excuse to make the trip."

"I'll go with you."

"We'll see. If not, what size shall I buy?"

"You don't know?" he said, laughing. "Why, *muy grande*, of course."

She reached between them and found him hardening again. "Unless they have a larger size than that," she said with a low, sensuous chuckle.

THE NIGHT PASSED as one of sweet challenge for Ry. All his instincts screamed at him to possess this woman in the most basic way, yet he managed to forestall his instincts, promising them full rein in less than twenty-four hours. It was backward from the way he'd always started a sexual relationship. The experimental part usually took place after the first wild coupling that joined two bodies. But he hadn't expected Freddy to show up in his room practically asking for a night of love, and there weren't drugstores on every corner out here in the desert.

Not that he was complaining. In fact, the lack of condoms gave him a wonderful excuse to learn every inch of her fantastic body, and she seemed inspired to do the same with him. He'd discovered he could bring her to completion simply by suckling her breasts. And as for him . . . she'd found some very creative ways of manipulating his lower anatomy to hurl him over the brink. They'd immersed themselves in the clawfoot bathtub where he'd had some interesting results with the running water, once he'd talked her into getting into a most provocative position. And he'd found out the potency that a few inches of lukewarm bathwater could add sloshing against him while she . . . He repressed the memory, which was having a predictable effect on him.

She'd just fallen asleep, and although it was nearly dawn, she might be able to catch an hour or so of rest. After all, he didn't want her to be too exhausted to enjoy tonight. Everything they'd done had been fun, but he still wanted . . . just wanted. He closed his eyes. He should sleep some, too. He wasn't an eighteen-year-old anymore, although last night he'd sure as hell felt like one. He touched her hand and her fingers curled around his in her sleep. With a smile of sweet exhaustion, he drifted off.

THE PHONE WOKE HIM to broad daylight and no Freddy. Dammit, he hadn't wanted her to sneak off like that, as if they'd been doing something shameful. And here he slept like a typical greenhorn long after the ranch day had officially begun.

He picked up the receiver impatiently and came close to snarling his greeting, until he realized it could be Freddy. "Yes?" he said.

"Mr. McGuinnes, this is Jose Ballesteros at Frontier Savings and Loan. There's a potentially disturbing development that may affect your financing on the True Love Guest Ranch. I started to discuss it with Miss Singleton earlier today, but she had to take care of another matter and will call me back. So I decided to call you."

Ry tensed. "What is it?"

"We have reason to believe there may be some petroleum drums buried on the property. E.P.A. standards being what they are these days, we'll have to locate those drums and ascertain the environmental risk before the sale can go through."

"Reason to believe?" Ry's eyes narrowed. "Who has reason to believe, and why?"

"Apparently, the environmental engineer who inspected the property yesterday talked to a neighbor, a Mr. Ebenezer Whitlock?"

Ry swore under his breath.

"Mr. Whitlock seems to remember that Mr. Singleton buried the tanks he used back in the days when he was fueling up his own vehicles, before the gas station was put in at La Osa."

"Are you aware that Whitlock had bid on the property, at a much lower figure than mine?"

"Well, yes, we are, but that doesn't change the situation. We need to talk to Miss Singleton to see if she can shed any light on the possibility of buried drums. But I wanted you to be aware, since you're staying at the ranch and she might bring it up."

"Don't have anybody call her. I'll handle it. We'll be in today with the information. How's that?"

"That...that would be fine, as long as you're sure that you and she won't get into any difficulties over—"

"Not at all. Thanks for the call, Mr. Ballesteros."

Ry showered, shaved and dressed with the speed inbred from years of working at a New York pace. He was standing in Freddy's office in less than twenty minutes, but the desk was occupied by Leigh, who was on the telephone.

"No, we're not blaming you, Mr. Gonzales," she said. "But it was the alfalfa we picked up last week, so you might want to check with some of your other customers." She glanced at Ry and held up one finger to indicate she'd soon be finished. "Yes, I think the horse will be fine. Freddy knows what she's doing. I'll keep you posted. Goodbye."

She replaced the receiver and gazed at him with speculation in her golden brown eyes. "Looking for Freddy?"

"Yes." He didn't evade her scrutiny. "Where is she?"

"Down at the corrals. One of the horses got into some moldy alfalfa and bloated. Want me to run you down there?"

"Yes." He didn't feel like being polite and making sure she wasn't too busy.

Leigh pushed her chair back. "Let's go."

She kept up with his rapid strides as they walked to her truck parked beside the ranch house. The crystal that hung from her rearview mirror flashed rainbows as they drove toward the corrals.

"Freddy's different this morning," Leigh said, looking straight ahead. "Do you happen to know anything about that?"

"Did you ask her?"

"Didn't have a chance. So I'm asking you."

Ry hesitated. But Leigh had been a friend to him so far, so he told her, "We spent the night together."

"I thought so. Been expecting it for days now."

Ry shook his head and chuckled. "Then you were way ahead of me."

"Haven't you heard that I'm psychic?"

"I thought that was with horses."

"Oh, I dabble in people, too. Besides, I know Freddy a little better than you. Or at least I did until last night," she amended with a smile. "You've probably caught up some by now."

Ry rolled down the window. It was getting warm in the cab. "We—ah—didn't spend a lot of time talking."

Leigh whooped and pounded on the steering wheel. "By God, Rycroft, you'll make a cowboy yet."

"Tell me about her, Leigh."

"Her love life, you mean?"

"Yes."

"She hasn't been serious about too many guys." Leigh paused. "Maybe I shouldn't assume it's serious between you two, either."

"Assume it."

She glanced at him. "I see. Well, her past loves, and there were only two she contemplated marrying, were both high-energy types like you. Like her, for that matter. Once you decided to stick around, I figured it was only a matter of time."

"What happened to those other high-energy types?"

"Oh, it usually boiled down to the same old argument in the end. Her whole mission in life has always been to run the True Love. None of the guys thought they'd enjoy hanging around to watch her do that." She glanced at him again. "Of course, with you, she has a different problem. You may want to run the ranch yourself."

"Not really." No, the problem was bigger than a mere power struggle, he thought.

"That's nice to know. Then maybe you could make a go of it. I'd like to see her find a man good enough for her."

He gave her a lopsided grin. "Are you implying I might be?"

"Maybe." She braked the truck to a stop under a mesquite and opened her door. "For a greenhorn, you're not so bad." She paused and turned back to him. "And I'll just bet you're dynamite in the sack," she added with a wink.

With a snort of laughter, Ry left the truck and followed Leigh to the same small corral where Red Devil had met his fate. Freddy stood inside, rubbing the nose of a small dun mare. Duane and Curtis hung over the side of the corral, along with a couple of the other hands.

Seeing Freddy sent a jolt of adrenaline through Ry, which mellowed into a misty-eyed tenderness as he drew closer. He was pretty sure what those reactions meant, although he and Freddy had been careful not to use the word last night. They might have abandoned themselves to each other physically, but emotions weren't so easily exposed for people like them. That was okay. They had some time.

He just hoped this petroleum drum business didn't become a major obstacle to the sale of the ranch. That could screw up a lot of his plans for the future, including his future with a certain dark-haired woman who was very inventive in the bedroom.

Duane turned as he and Leigh approached. "She's doin' okay," he said, reaching for his can of tobacco in his hip pocket.

Freddy pushed herself to her feet and turned, her eyes widening slightly when she saw Ry. "I think she'll be fine now." She picked up her kit of medical supplies and handed it across the fence to Curtis. Then she walked over to lean against the gate to the corral. "Did you call Gonzales?" she asked Leigh.

She looked tired, Ry thought with a pang of guilt.

"Yep," Leigh replied. "He was upset, but I told him we weren't holding him responsible. And I warned him to check with anybody else who bought some of that grain."

Freddy nodded. "Good." Her gaze traveled to Ry and she smiled gently.

The smile made him dizzy. He longed to whisk her off to some private spot and soothe away the lines of fatigue shadowing those sage-colored eyes.

"Then I guess we'd all better get back to work," Duane said, slipping a plug of tobacco under his lip.

Curtis glanced at Duane's tobacco can as he shoved it back into his hip pocket, where a permanent faded circle had been formed by the pressure of the can. "Did I ever tell you folks about the New York City gal who wanted to go to bed with a cowboy?" Curtis started to laugh at his own joke and pointed to the impression of the tobacco can in Duane's pocket. "When she saw the size of their condoms, she plum chickened out!" Curtis slapped his thigh and chortled.

Ry's shoulders shook with laughter. One glance into Freddy's eyes, brimming with helpless merriment, and he looked away, across the corrals. If he shared this joke too intimately with her, the whole crowd would know what Leigh knew, and he wasn't ready to go that public yet.

"Thank you, Curtis," Freddy said, opening the corral gate and walking out to join them. "I don't know how we'd make it around here without a few of your jokes to keep us going."

"Nothin' to it," Curtis said over his shoulder as he headed for the tack shed.

"Well, I'm due to take some German folks out for a trail ride in a half hour," Leigh said. "Freddy, I assume you can give Ry a lift back to the house?"

Freddy looked at Ry. "You didn't come down here to ride Red Devil?"

"I came down here to see you."

"Oh." She lowered her eyes and a faint dusting of pink tinged her cheeks.

"Come on, Duane," Leigh said, grabbing the grizzled cowboy's arm as he stood gaping at Freddy and Ry. "You and I have horses to saddle and dudes to entertain."

"Shore, Leigh." Duane followed Leigh, but he stopped several times to glance over his shoulder.

Freddy gazed up at Ry with a captivating shyness lurking in her eyes. "Nothing stays private long at the True Love, I'm afraid."

"That's okay." He traced the line of her jaw with one finger. "I got up this morning and expected the news to be written across my forehead. Which reminds me, why did you leave without waking me up?"

"You looked so peaceful, and I knew there was nothing you absolutely had to do, so I let you sleep."

"While you had to get up and work. I feel like a selfish jerk."

"Don't." She laid a hand on his arm, then abruptly took it away, as if the contact had burned her fingers.

"Be careful," he teased. "I'm barely in control of myself as it is."

The shyness had left her eyes. "Me too, cowboy," she murmured in the sexiest voice he'd ever heard.

The sensual impact of the stoked fire in her gaze took his breath away. He struggled to remember why he'd needed to see her. Nothing seemed as important as what he was contemplating right now, and that involved naked bodies and soft sheets.

"Shall we go back to the house, then?" she asked. "I have a call I need to return."

Of course, he thought. The phone call. "That's what I came to talk to you about. Ballesteros called me after he tried to talk to you. He wants to know what you can tell him about old petroleum drums buried on the property."

She frowned. "There aren't any. Dad had them all dug up and hauled away when the gas station was built in La Osa."

"Then why the hell is Eb Whitlock telling the environmental engineer they're still down there?"

Freddy looked startled. "He did?"

"Yesterday. And unless I miss my guess, this is a deliberate tactic on his part to keep my partners and me from buying the ranch."

"That's stooping pretty low, Ry. I can believe he'd carry on about the curse to discourage you, but lie about petroleum drums? I doubt it."

Her defense of Whitlock irritated him. Whitlock wasn't really a rival, but Ry wished Freddy would be a little less generous with her opinion of the guy. "Then I'd appreciate it if you'd set him straight. Unless you want to help him in his obstructionist cause." He paused, then said, "Maybe I should ask that first, and not make any faulty assumptions. How do you stand on my purchase of the True Love?"

Hurt shone from her hazel eyes. "Do you really have to ask?"

He was instantly contrite and reached for her. "I'm sorry. Really sorry," he said, pouring his heart into his gaze. "If you still wanted to stop me, last night wouldn't have happened."

"No, it wouldn't."

So now she trusted him, with herself and her ranch, which were almost the same thing. He felt a sharp stab of guilt that she still didn't know his ultimate plans. He'd look for a good time to tell her and make her see that selling the ranch was the most sensible course of action for everyone concerned. Somehow, he'd work through her initial resistance to the idea. He had to. Too much was at stake now.

"We'll go to the house and call Eb," she said. "I'm sure this is a big misunderstanding."

Ry didn't think so, but he kept his opinion to himself this time. He'd love to be proven wrong.

13

WHEN FREDDY ENTERED her office and walked around behind her desk, Ry remained leaning in the doorway, his hat shoved to the back of his head. They hadn't talked much on the way back to the ranch house, as if each knew an argument could easily break out over the subject of Eb's character.

She picked up the receiver and glanced at him. "I know what you think, but Eb would not say something like this unless he believed it was true."

Ry's expression gave nothing away, but he didn't agree with her, either.

Freddy punched in the Whitlocks' number. She knew it by heart. She'd spent hours over there as a child, back when Eb's wife, Loraine, was still alive. Eb and Loraine had been childless, and so they'd become honorary aunt and uncle to the Singleton girls, especially after Freddy and Leigh's mother died. Ry didn't know all that history, and besides, he was from New York. New Yorkers were famous for their suspicious natures.

Eb's housekeeper, Doreen, answered the phone. "Sure, I'll get him, honey," she said. "He's just out back working on the horseshoe pit he wanted to put in before the next party."

Freddy smiled. Eb loved to entertain, and he usually invited at least a hundred people. His barbecued beef was legendary in the valley.

In a few moments, his voice boomed into her ear. "Freddy! Gonzales called me about that alfalfa. Your horse okay? I meant to phone you, but I got distracted. Which one was it?"

"Tumbleweed, our little dun mare, and she'll be okay. Luckily, we got to her in time."

"I found mold in my alfalfa, too, but I hadn't given any to my horses, thank God," Eb said. "Gonzales is giving us credit on a new load, of course. I made sure he'd do that for all of us."

"Thanks, Eb. Listen, I understand you talked to the environmental engineer who was out here yesterday."

"Just happened to run into him while I was out riding fence. Nice fella. Hated to tell him about those drums, but he was asking questions, and I'm a lousy liar."

"Well, I think your memory's playing tricks on you, Eb." Freddy put a smile in her voice. "Dad had those hauled out when we stopped using them. Nothing's buried at the True Love."

"Freddy, you were only a little thing then. I believe I remember better than you do. He decided not to go to the expense. We didn't have so many regulations back then, of course."

"I was ten years old, Eb, and I remember the trucks coming in to haul them away."

A cajoling note came into Eb's voice. "I would do anything for you. You know that. But I have to tell the truth. Those drums are still there."

"Eb, they're not, either!"

"Well, I hope you have some paperwork to prove it, sweetheart, or somebody will have a little digging to do."

Freddy sighed. "I'll look through the files. Talk to you later, Eb."

"Good luck. By the way, you and Leigh are coming to the party next week, aren't you?"

"We'll be there," she said. "Goodbye now." She replaced the receiver and stared at the phone. "I *know* Dad had the drums taken out."

"I'm sure he did, too," Ry said from the doorway. "Old Whitlock's trying to screw up the deal."

She glared at him. "Stop assuming that, Ry! We're talking about something that happened twenty-two years ago. He could have forgotten, and in all honesty thinks he's telling the truth."

Ry folded his arms. "Pretty convenient that he happened to run into the engineer yesterday, wouldn't you say?"

"He was checking his fence for breaks. Is that a crime?"

"I wouldn't think a fellow of Whitlock's stature would be inspecting his own fence. Doesn't he have hired hands to do that?"

Freddy pushed away from the desk and rounded it to open a file cabinet drawer. "You have to understand old cowboys. They can't sit around, and sometimes the most satisfying work is the most mundane. I can easily imagine Eb worrying about his own fence. Now, if I can just find some record of those drums being hauled away, we'll take it into town and clear up this business once and for all."

"You think there might be a receipt in there?"

She shoved the stuffed files apart. "I think there might be."

"Looks like you could use a second file cabinet."

"You're right. But I'd have to find another battered one like this, so they'd match. A brand-new one would spoil the ambience."

He laughed and walked over to brace one arm against the top of the cabinet. "At least we have a great excuse to go into town today," he said in a low voice.

Heat washed over her, but she kept her head down as she closed one drawer and opened another. "Do you think so?"

"When I first came down to the corrals and saw you, I completely forgot about Ballesteros. And you know how important this deal is to me. But one look at you, and all I could remember was last night."

Freddy realized her hands had stilled and she'd been staring sightlessly at the mashed files for several seconds.

"I've never spent a night like that in my life, Freddy."

She risked looking into his eyes. What she saw there made her grip the edges of the file cabinet to keep from throwing herself into his arms. She swallowed. "You'd better go find something to do for a few minutes or I'll never finish this search."

The corner of his mouth tilted up.

"I mean it, Ry. And don't forget, this office is in the middle of all the activity around here. People come and go constantly. We may not be able to keep our relationship a secret, but I'd rather not flaunt it."

He smiled softly. "You're right. Another five seconds and I'm liable to throw you down on the floor and rip your clothes off."

She believed every word of it. "Take a hike, cowboy."

He tipped his hat. "I'll be on the front porch," he drawled.

A half hour later, Freddy gave up. If the receipt was in the bulging file cabinet, she wouldn't be able to find it without going through every piece of paper in every aging folder. That could take hours, even if she enlisted some help. She went looking for Ry and found him sitting with Dexter and Chloe, Dexter's dog.

"It's like the old needle in a haystack," she said, dropping into a chair next to Ry. "I tried all the logical places, but no luck."

"Dexter remembers the drums were hauled away," Ry said.

Freddy leaned around Ry. "You do? The day those big trucks came and took the drums, the ones Dad used for gas?"

Dexter nodded. "Yep."

"I sure wish Eb Whitlock remembered it."

Dexter made a face.

"Oh, Dex!" Despite her frustration, Freddy laughed. "You just don't like him because he kissed Belinda." She glanced at Ry. "Let's go see Mr. Ballesteros. On the way, I'll try to remember the name of the trucking company. They might have records. Do you remember the name, Dexter?"

"Nope. Used to."

"Yeah, me too." Freddy reached across Ry's ankles to pat the dog. "See you later, Chloe."

"Chloe," Dexter said, nodding. "That's it. That's her name."

"What about Duane?" Ry asked. "Has he been here long enough to remember the trucking company?"

"No, but Belinda has." Freddy jumped up and headed for the kitchen.

"I'll come with you," Ry said.

But to Freddy's disappointment, Belinda had been too busy with cooking chores back then to take note of the removal of the drums.

"Let's drive in and see Ballesteros," Ry suggested as they left the kitchen. "Maybe he'd take a notarized statement from you."

Hope filtered through her gloom. "You think so?"

"It's worth a shot."

"Okay." She took her leather purse from a bottom drawer of the desk. "Let's go."

Ry looked surprised. "That's it? You don't have to fix your face, or anything?"

She paused in confusion. "Why, do I have a smudge of dirt on my nose?"

"No, you're perfect, but I've never known a woman who'd walk right out the door without taking time to primp a little."

Freddy hooked her purse over her arm and grinned at him. "That's because you're used to city girls. Welcome to the country, greenhorn."

THEY TOOK Freddy's truck into town. "Let's hit the drugstore first," Ry said. "I don't want to forget the most important part of this trip."

"As if you would."

He loved the warm color on her cheeks and wondered if he could intensify it. "Actually, there's no chance I'll forget. There is a chance I'll try to seduce you somewhere along the way, and I want to be prepared." As he'd hoped, she blushed even pinker.

"Ry, for heaven's sake. It's broad daylight and we're heading into the heart of the city."

"Which presents a challenge, I'll admit, but I'm getting used to that with you."

She wheeled the truck into the parking lot of a strip shopping center that contained a chain drugstore. "Okay, Mr. One-Track Mind. If you'll make the purchase, I'll use that pay phone to call Ballesteros and tell him we're on our way. It's getting close to lunchtime and we don't want to sit and cool our heels waiting for him."

"Good point."

Moments later, he returned to the truck with a small plastic bag. "All set with Ballesteros?"

She leaned one arm against the steering wheel and gave him an assessing glance. "If I didn't know better, I'd say you planned this, but I guess it would have been virtually impossible, even for a man of your imagination."

"I don't understand what you're talking about."

"Ballesteros has left for lunch, and after lunch, he has an appointment that will keep him occupied until two."

Awareness flickered in his blue eyes. "Really?"

"We could drive home and come back, but that would take almost an hour by itself."

"I see." Ry turned casually and peered down the road. "I could take you to lunch."

"That's a possibility."

He pointed to a hotel a few blocks down the road. "Ever been there for lunch?"

"They don't have a restaurant."

He turned back to her, his gaze intense. "Exactly."

Tension coiled within her. "Ry, I've never checked into a hotel for two hours in the middle of the day. I'd feel like—"

"Someone's lover?" He didn't touch her, but his glance caressed her with bold intimacy. "You are."

Her fingers trembled as she turned the key in the ignition. "I suppose you're used to this sort of interlude, a big-city boy like you." She checked the rearview mirror and backed out of the parking space.

"Right. Two-hour lunches with the well-stacked secretary are commonplace with me."

She hit the brake. "They are?"

He chuckled. "No, Freddy."

She pulled into traffic with the deliberate care of someone who'd had one too many drinks, which was the way she felt—high. "But I'll bet you've done this before."

"I think I can handle the registration and checkout without blushing, if that's what you mean," he said.

"Won't they ask you about luggage, and when you'll be checking out, and stuff like that?"

"I'll tell them the luggage is in the truck and we'll be checking out in the morning. Then when we leave, I'll explain that we had a sudden change of plans."

"But they'll *know*. The maids will see the bed's been . . ."

"Well-used?" he supplied.

She nodded as her heart pounded furiously.

"Does that mean you'd rather find a coffee shop and have lunch?"

She took a deep breath. "No." She flipped on her turn signal and swept into the hotel's drive-through entrance.

"Want to come in with me while I get us the room?" he asked.

"No."

He chuckled again. "Be right back."

Freddy sat in the truck trying to figure out what she'd say if anyone came by who recognized her sitting there in plain sight with the True Love Guest Ranch brand on the truck's door panels. She ran a guest ranch. Why would she be parked at a hotel in town? She thought for a minute. She was . . . comparing room rates. That was it. She and a friend were checking out the going rates in

Tucson, to decide if their own pricing structure was reasonable.

But no one came by, and within minutes Ry was back, a key in one hand. "Drive around behind the place," he said, climbing in. "I thought you'd rather not park the truck where anyone on the road could recognize it."

Freddy let out a breath. "Thank you."

"I want to give you pleasure, not embarrassment."

Pleasure. The word echoed in her mind as they parked the truck in the nearly deserted lot behind the hotel. The rooms all opened to the outside, and Ry guided her toward one on the ground floor, put the key in the lock and opened the door. She stepped into the cool interior with a shiver of anticipation.

Behind her, the lock clicked into place and the curtains swished closed, throwing the room into twilight. The air conditioner hummed in a unit beneath the window. In front of her was a king-size bed, quilted spread neatly tucked under the pillows. Now that they were here, alone and undetected, the thrill of being sinful took hold.

"Stay there," she said to Ry, her command coming out in a sultry murmur, "while I redecorate."

"Be my guest."

She laid her hat on the built-in that held the television set as she walked past it to the far side of the bed. In one movement, she swept back the spread and the top sheet, destroying the atmosphere of neatness. Then she plumped the pillows against the headboard.

"Finished?" Ry stood watching her with his thumbs hooked through his belt loops.

"Just getting started." She reached down and pulled off her boots. "Do you come into town often, cowboy?" she asked as she began undoing the snaps on her shirt.

"Not often enough, obviously."

"Gets lonely out on the trail, I imagine." She held his gaze while she popped the snaps at her wrists and took the shirt off with sensuous rolls of her shoulders.

"You can't imagine how lonely." Passion blazed in his eyes.

She unbuckled her belt and pulled it slowly through the loops. "Days without the soft comfort of a woman's body can take its toll on a man."

"It can make him crazy."

"And are you going crazy?" The jeans slithered over her hips and she kicked them away.

His reply was husky. "Insane."

"Good." She unhooked her bra. "That's how I like my men."

"So I figured."

She dropped the bra to the floor and cupped her breasts. "How long has it been since you touched a woman?"

"Too long."

"Well, I hope you have some staying power." She smoothed her hands down her rib cage, hooked her thumbs in the elastic of her panties and tugged them down her body in one continuous motion. "I'd hate for everything to be over prematurely." She held her panties dangling by two fingers. "If you know what I mean." Then she tossed them across the room toward him.

He caught them without taking his gaze from hers. "I don't think you'll have any complaints."

"Now, that sounds promising." She stretched out on the bed and propped her cheek on her fist. "Would you care to make good on that boast, cowboy?"

He took off his hat and dropped her panties into the crown before setting the hat next to hers on the built-in. "Reckon I would."

He leaned against the built-in to pull off his boots. Then he rounded the end of the bed, working on his shirt buttons as he walked. She lay back against the pillows as he came to stand beside her and placed the box of condoms at the precise center of the bedside table. "Your underwear was damp," he said.

Her heartbeat thundered in her ears. "Is that so? I wonder what could have caused that?"

He unbuckled his belt and gave her a tight smile. "I think we're about to find out, *Liebchen.*"

"A cowboy who can speak German. Oh, my." Freddy ran her tongue over her dry lips as he eased the zipper past the bulge of his arousal. Her heart was chugging like a freight train going up a rise, and the ache within her grew with each bit of magnificent man Ry revealed. When his manhood sprung free, so ready for her, she sucked in her breath.

All his clothes gone, he placed a knee on the bed and leaned toward her. "Is that how you want me to make love to you, little lady? In German?"

"No, cowboy," she murmured, reaching to cup his face and pull him down for a long-awaited kiss. "I want to understand every word you say."

But he didn't need many words to tell her how much he wanted her. Braced above her, he roved her face and neck with his hungry lips. She arched upward to receive his kisses at her breasts. His touch had already become achingly familiar, and she responded with lush abandon as he stroked her hips, her thighs, the backs of her knees. When he caressed her between her thighs, he

groaned softly. "I think we've found out why your panties were drenched, *chérie*."

She gasped with longing and gripped his shoulders as
he probed deep. "Love me, Ry."

He braced his elbow beside her head as he reached for
the box. "And what else did you ask for?" he murmured
in her ear. "Staying power?"

"That might not . . . be necessary."

"Ah, but it would be more fun." He nibbled at the lobe
of her ear. "Help me with this, *chérie*. I want to feel your
hands on me."

She took the packet and ripped it open with shaking
fingers. Then he whispered instructions in her ear as she
fumbled with the task, bringing them both to a fever
pitch of excitement. Finally, she managed, and in a
breathless voice announced her success.

His response was hoarse with need as he moved between her thighs. "Never has incompetence felt so good."
Poised above her, he smoothed her hair back from her
face. "We've made love in so many ways, but this was
what I really wanted." He eased forward. "This."

"Yes." She lifted her hips to meet him, tension throb-
bing through her, demanding release. "Please, Ry."

He slipped both hands beneath her hips, and with a
sharp intake of breath he plunged deep. At that first
thrust she erupted into a dazzling climax, calling his
name as she writhed in his arms. He moved with each
spasm, heightening her pleasure until she became delir-
ious with sensation.

Gradually, she regained the ability to breathe, and her
heartbeat slowed a fraction. Yet he was still within her,
the sweet pressure producing tiny aftershocks, and a re-

newed curl of tension. She looked up to find him smiling gently as he gazed at her.

"Good?" he asked.

"Oh, yes." Good didn't begin to describe the pleasure he'd given her, but she had no idea how to tell him that she'd never reacted so quickly and thoroughly with anyone.

"There's more." Lacing his fingers through hers, he stretched her arms above her head, lifting her breasts for his mouth. Nuzzling her pert nipples, he began a slow rhythm with his hips.

Each sensuous thrust set off a responding pulse beat within her, fueled even more by the flick of his warm tongue against her breasts. Sanity slipped away again, to be replaced by the ever-tightening grasp of need. He had pleasured her well the night before, but now he touched elements far more basic as he again and again probed her moist center, claiming his place there. With a cry of surrender, she arched upward as he pushed her once more into the shattering world of release.

Before she'd completely recovered, he wrapped his arms around her waist and rolled to his back, carrying her with him and holding her tightly locked against him. She braced her hands on his chest and absorbed his hot gaze as it traveled over her breasts and down to the juncture of their thighs. He glanced back up into her eyes.

"Love me," he murmured. "Ride me, *chérie*."

With a smile of female anticipation, she rose slightly on her knees and settled back down over his heated shaft. He moaned. Her palms flat against his chest, she repeated the motion in a faster rhythm. He clutched the sheet in both hands as his breathing grew labored. Faster she moved, and faster, until he was gasping. She gave him no mercy. She wanted his surrender to be as complete as hers.

His shout of release seemed torn from his soul. As she leaned down to kiss him, he looked into her eyes and she knew he was hers.

14

AT FIVE MINUTES before two, Ry and Freddy walked into the lobby of Frontier Savings and Loan. He'd assured her that after a shower at the hotel and the use of a comb and lipstick from her purse, she didn't look as if she'd just spent two hours making love.

More specifically, a stranger wouldn't know it, he amended to himself as he ushered her past a large Remington sculpture of a cattle stampede and over to a cluster of desks to the right of the teller windows. He had only to gaze into her languorous eyes to read the aftermath of passion written there. The merest brush of her sleeve against his and scenes flashed through his mind— Freddy tossing her underwear across the room, Freddy stretching out on the bed and inviting him to make good on his boast, Freddy arching in surrender at the moment of climax. They'd discovered paradise in that hotel room, and he still carried a bit of it with him.

"We'll wait," Freddy said, nudging him. "Won't we, Mr. McGuinnes?"

He snapped out of his daze long enough to realize Freddy had been communicating with the loan officer at the desk nearest Ballesteros's empty one. And Ry had been out to lunch—literally. He cleared his throat. "Of course."

"Would either of you care for coffee?" the woman asked.

He glanced at Freddy, who shook her head. "No, thanks," he said. "We'll just have a seat until Mr. Ballesteros arrives." Ry wondered if Ballesteros was engaged in a little rendezvous of his own. Probably not. Just because Ry was in an erotic fog didn't mean everyone else was.

As they sat in imitation-leather chairs, Freddy leaned toward him. "You'll have to sharpen up, there, McGuinnes," she said in a low voice. "If you stand around staring off into space, people will wonder what you've been up to."

He gave her a crooked smile. "You're a powerful force, Miss Singleton. I'm not sure I realized what I was letting myself in for."

"Ah." She studied him, a wary look in her eyes. "Second thoughts?"

"Yes. I was trying to figure out how we could have managed this meeting with simply a phone call so we wouldn't have had to leave the room."

Her lips curved provocatively. He wanted to kiss off every bit of her newly applied lipstick.

"Miss Singleton? Mr. McGuinnes? I'm Jose Ballesteros. Sorry to keep you waiting."

Ry looked up as a short, round man with an olive complexion held out his hand. Apparently, they'd missed his entrance into the building. They really would have to pay better attention to the world around them.

"No problem." Ry stood and shook his hand firmly.

Freddy followed suit, and Ballesteros took a seat behind his cluttered desk. "Were you able to find out anything about the petroleum drums?" he asked, pawing through the papers on his desk.

"The drums were taken out," Freddy said, leaning forward. "I was there. I saw the trucks loaded with the drums pull away and drive down the road."

"Well, that's good," Ballesteros said cautiously, glancing up at her. "Do you have any documentation as to when that was done?"

Ry shifted in his seat. "We're running into some difficulty with that and we thought you might be able to take a notarized statement from Miss Singleton."

Ballesteros met his gaze. "Not a good idea. We can do that, but she'd have to sign a statement that she's responsible for anything that's found buried there, ever. That kind of liability is too broad, in my opinion."

"You're right." Ry shook his head in frustration. "I guess we have to find that receipt."

"What if we don't?" Freddy asked.

"Then I'm afraid, in order to get financing, we have to dig."

"Who's we?" she persisted.

"Well . . ." Ballesteros obviously wasn't enjoying his role as the bearer of bad news. "The present owners claim they have no responsibility in the matter, and technically they don't. I'm afraid the expense of either proving the drums aren't there, or getting them out and cleaning up the area if they are, will fall to the person who was the owner at the time the drums were installed."

Ry had figured that one out, but he wanted Ballesteros to deliver the message instead of him. And he wanted her to realize just what a jerk Whitlock was turning out to be.

"So, since my father and mother are dead, the responsibility falls to me," Freddy said in a surprisingly calm voice.

Ballesteros steepled his fingers. "I'm afraid so. If I were you, I'd do everything I could to find a receipt or locate the trucking company. In the meantime, the financing decisions will be put on hold. I'm sorry. This is a very hot subject right now. And you'd better hope that if the drums are down there, they didn't pollute the water supply."

"They're not down there," Freddy said, an edge to her voice.

"Let's hope not."

Ry stood. "We'll find a way to prove it. Thanks for your time."

As they left the building in a much less euphoric mood than when they'd arrived, Ry reflected that there was nothing that spoiled paradise quicker than a snake.

On the way back to the True Love, he glanced at Freddy's rigid profile. "Now do you see what your friend and neighbor has done? He's not only thrown a monkey wrench into the sale, he may have set you up for a very costly procedure."

"Which I couldn't begin to pay for on what I make as foreman of the ranch."

"You won't pay for it. I will."

"That's crazy. It's not your responsibility, and it's bad business besides! I won't let you do that."

"I want the ranch, Freddy." *And the foreman, if she'll have me.* "Whitlock may think this will discourage me from pursuing the sale, but he's mistaken."

"I still can't believe that Eb—"

"Be realistic, Freddy. This was all calculated by him. He knows the drums aren't there, but my partners and I don't. If you can't pay to have it checked out, then we'd have to, and we have no idea what sort of pollution problem we might run into. Any logical businessperson would back out of a sale with that sort of snag. If the drums have polluted the groundwater, the property's value will drop drastically."

"But none of that's true!"

"I know, and the one thing Whitlock didn't count on was that I'd credit the memory of a ten-year-old girl over that of a grown man."

Her voice softened. "And you do?"

"Absolutely."

"Thank you."

"Don't thank me," he said with a chuckle. "It makes sense. A couple of weeks ago, you would have resorted to almost anything, including rumors of buried petroleum drums, to scare me off the True Love. If you really wanted Whitlock to have the property, you'd agree the stuff was down there, and I'd ride off into the sunset."

Her throat moved convulsively. "I guess I don't want that anymore."

"Good." His heart squeezed. She hadn't made a passionate declaration, but it was a beginning. He had a long way to go, however, and he still hadn't confessed his plans for selling the property. Guilt nagged him, but caution held him back. Before he confessed, he wanted her to care more about him than she did about the True Love Ranch.

THERE WERE four drawers in the aging file cabinet. Freddy directed Ry to pull them all out and carry them to the dining room, where no one would need the tables for at least two hours. She called Leigh down at the corrals and asked her to come up and help. Then she enlisted Belinda, so there was one person to a drawer.

"Anything that looks like a trucking company receipt, or a hauling receipt, or trash removal, or anything remotely sounding as if it could be what we need, sing out," Freddy said as they began the search.

An hour and a half later, several possibilities had been found then discarded. The tables were piled with folders, and the drawers were almost empty. Leigh slapped her hand on the table in frustration. "Eb Whitlock is a horse's ass! I have half a mind to ride over there and tell him so."

"He's just being an aggressive businessman," Ry said. "Unfortunately for his plans, he's also dealing with one. I'll call in the morning and get somebody out here with a backhoe. Can you pinpoint the location for me, Freddy?"

Freddy's chest tightened with anxiety. "I sure hope so."

He frowned. "What do you mean, you hope so? If he had gas pumps, the drums would be right under that area, so you must remember where the pumps were."

"I do. Somewhere behind the big corral."

"Somewhere behind the big corral?"

Tears threatened. She'd been on an emotional roller coaster for too many days, and it was taking a toll. "I was ten, Ry! I don't remember exactly."

He rose from his chair. "Hey, it's okay." He crossed the room and wrapped his arms around her, in full view of Leigh and Belinda. "We'll dig up whatever we have to in order to satisfy those creeps."

She started to struggle away, but he held her tight. "Belinda and Leigh don't care if I give you a hug," he said gently. "And you look like you could use one."

"Hey, kiss her if you want," Leigh said. "It's been a long afternoon."

Ry chuckled. "I just might."

"Don't worry," Belinda said. "I think I can remember where the pumps were. And Dexter can remember, too. We'll find the right spot."

"Somebody's talking about me."

Freddy peeked over Ry's shoulder. Dexter stood in the doorway of the dining room. Balanced on his walker, he surveyed the stacks of files with disapproval. "What a mess!"

"We're trying to find the receipt from that trucking company," Freddy said.

"They are." Dexter swept an arm toward Leigh and his wife. "You're not."

Freddy laughed. "No, I'm hugging Ry."

Dexter nodded. "Good."

"Yeah." Freddy leaned back and smiled into Ry's face. "He's one of the good guys."

"That's it!" Dexter exclaimed, clomping into the room with his walker. "Good guys! Good guys!"

Freddy disentangled herself to turn and stare at Dexter.

"Dragging!" Dexter said, obviously very excited. "No, lifting! Big. Real big! Round! Thataway!" He pointed in the direction of the road.

Leigh pushed herself up from the table, her attention focused on Dexter. "Are you talking about the drums, Dex?"

"Yeah! Good guys!"

Disappointment swept over Freddy. She had thought maybe Dexter was remembering something significant, when he was only making a comment about the men who had done the hauling. Apparently, he'd liked them. "I'm sure they were good guys, Dexter. But we need the name of the company."

Belinda jumped up so fast, she knocked over her chair. "That *was* the name of the company. There was a trucking company back then that called themselves Good Guys!"

With a gasp, Freddy ran for the Yellow Pages. She hurried back, flipping through the book. Then her shoulders sagged again. There was no Good Guys Trucking Company. "I guess they've gone out of business."

"Or somebody else bought them out," Ry said, reaching for the book. "Give me a few minutes in your office, *chérie.*"

"Ooh la-la!" Leigh said as he left the room. "Big sister, my hat's off to you for catching a stud who speaks French."

"Good Guys," Dexter said again, nodding. "I remembered."

"Yes, you did." Freddy walked over and squeezed his arm. "It's not your fault they're out of business."

Belinda started reloading files into a drawer. "We'll have to clean this up pretty quick. Dinnertime's almost here."

"Right," Freddy agreed. She and Leigh lifted stacks of files and settled them in the drawers. Leigh started to pick up a drawer that was full. "Let Ry do that when he comes back," Freddy said.

Leigh set the drawer down with a grin. "My, how quickly you've become used to having a big, strong man around."

Freddy gazed at her sister. "It's a little scary, isn't it?"

"I think it's lovely," Belinda said, patting her last files into place. "Now, I'd better go see how everyone's coming along in the kitchen."

"Thanks, Belinda," Freddy said. "We couldn't have—"

"I found them!" Ry strode into the room waving a piece of paper. "Cunningham Trucking bought out Good Guys sixteen years ago."

Freddy was almost afraid to ask. "But do they have any records that go back that far?"

Ry's jubilant grin provided the answer. "The senior Mr. Cunningham saves everything, according to a disgruntled secretary. She promised she would have no trouble locating the receipt, and she was glad that there was some justification, at long last, for keeping all those dusty files. I gave her your fax number. She expects to send it within the hour."

Freddy had hurled herself into his arms before she realized it. She kissed him soundly and whirled away to pump Dexter's arm. "You did it," she said, grinning at both of them. "What a team."

Both Dexter and Ry looked immensely pleased with themselves. Ry turned to the old man and held out his hand. Dexter shook it with enthusiasm.

Leigh sauntered up, eyes sparkling. "Congratulations, and all that. But it's time to get back to work, Ry, my friend. Freddy says you're the man to call when it comes to hefting file drawers, and we'll have dinner guests coming in any minute now."

"No problem. I'll—"

"In fact," Leigh said, glancing around Ry, "someone just came through the front door with a suitcase. Freddy, were we expecting another guest tonight?"

"Not that I know of." She looked at the man silhouetted against the open doorway, a battered suitcase in his hand and a cowboy hat on his head. "Maybe he's looking for a job," she said in a low tone. "I'll go see."

But before she could approach the stranger, he plunked down his suitcase and strode into the dining room, his boot heels hitting the pine floor with a confident thump. "T.R., is that you? Didn't recognize you without your briefcase and three-piece suit."

Ry turned in surprise, and his eyes widened. "Lavette! Where did you come from? Why didn't you let us know you were heading in?"

"Thought I'd surprise you." He shook Ry's hand.

Freddy assessed the man's clothes, dusty but new, and smiled. Another urban cowboy had arrived. He looked less than thirty years old, with a devilish gleam in his green eyes and a dimple in his cheek. Thick dark hair reached to his collar. She was already figuring out which horse to put him on, when Ry turned to her.

"Chase Lavette, I'd like you to meet Freddy Singleton, the foreman," he said.

"Glad to meet you." He offered his hand in a firm grip.

"And Freddy's sister, Leigh Singleton, the head wrangler," Ry added.

Leigh responded to his handshake with a smile. "Welcome to the True Love. Do you speak French, Mr. Lavette?"

"Nope." His grin was disarming. "I only know how to kiss that way."

"Easy, Lavette," Ry said, winking at Leigh. "These women can rope and hog-tie you in under thirty seconds if you're disrespectful."

Chase touched the brim of his hat. "No disrespect intended. Can't afford it with my back."

"How's the healing coming along?" Ry asked.

"Pretty well. Sometimes I have good days, sometimes not so good. Today's been good, so far."

"What'd you do, walk from New York?" Ry asked, peering at the dust on his friend's clothes.

"Just from the main road. Hitched from the airport, for the fun of it. If I'd had a saddle on my shoulder, it would've been perfect." Chase laughed. "I see what you mean about the way the city's moving in this direction, McGuinnes. This land is solid gold."

As if in slow motion, Freddy looked at Ry. She saw the flash of panic in his eyes and her heart began to freeze. Then he turned from her and put his hand on Chase's shoulder, as if to guide him away.

But Chase seemed determined to deliver his observations, oblivious to the dead silence that had settled over the room. "I'm sure that before long, this will be a subdivision, like you predicted, T.R., so I figured bad back or not, I'd better get out here and enjoy the place while I can."

FREDDY BROKE and ran. She and Ry had left the truck parked in front of the ranch house, and the keys were on the floor, where she always put them. She heard a shout as she gunned the engine to life. Slamming her foot to the floor, she peeled out, glancing in the rearview mirror. She'd covered Ry in a shower of dust. She considered backing up and running him over.

The tears didn't start until she reached the corrals and started saddling Maureen. Fortunately, she could saddle and bridle the mare blindfolded, so it didn't matter that she was crying so hard she couldn't see. Duane came over when she was nearly done.

"Freddy, darlin', what's the matter?" he asked, more tenderly than she'd remembered Duane ever speaking in his life.

"Sorry," she said, her voice choked. "Can't talk about it."

"Gonna ride it out?"

"Yep."

"Be careful. Don't poke Maureen's leg in no gopher holes 'cause you're not lookin'. And hold on. Don't want to hafta scrape you off of no barrel cactus, neither."

"I'll be careful." Freddy vaulted into the saddle and slapped Maureen's rump with the reins. As if the little mare understood the need for haste, she took off at a lope.

Freddy sent Maureen down the path leading toward the wash. Branches whipped past, and Freddy ducked under them, anchoring her hat to her head with one hand as she drove her heels into Maureen's sides, urging her on. Maybe if she rode fast enough, she could outrun her thoughts. Maybe if she cried hard enough, her tears would wash away the pain of betrayal.

Maureen took the descent to the sandy wash in one graceful leap. A less experienced rider might have pitched forward and sent the mare to her knees, throwing the rider headfirst into the wash. Freddy anticipated the weight change and glided with Maureen to the dry bed. She leaned over and whispered into Maureen's velvet ear, "Run like hell, baby."

Maureen's haunches bunched and she bolted as if from a racetrack gate. Freddy kept her body low over the horse's neck, relishing the snap of the mare's mane against her wet cheeks. Her hair worked its way loose from the clip, which tumbled to the sand as her tresses rippled like a flag in the wind. Maureen's hooves pounded the dry creek bed, sending up grainy geysers as she stretched her legs in a dead run.

The hot wind dried Freddy's tears as soon as they fell, and the fierce joy of riding full speed partly replaced the pain in her heart. But the late-afternoon sun beat down on her shoulders, and she realized that no matter what she needed, she couldn't expect Maureen to continue at this pace for long. Already the mare's breathing was labored, her neck dark with sweat. The wash narrowed, and Freddy pulled gently on the reins, slowing the animal to a lope. A hundred yards farther on, she guided Maureen into a trot, and finally slowed her to a walk.

"Thanks, girl." Freddy cleared the residue of emotion from her throat and patted the horse's lathered neck. "I'll make it up to you. I promise I will." Then, with a whimper, she laid her cheek on the wind-whipped mane. "Once a city slicker, always a city slicker, Maureen. Don't ever forget it." New tears threatened, and she sniffed them back. "No more tears. No more tears for Mr. T. R. McGuinnes."

But she had to think what to do. He would buy the ranch, he and his city slicker friends. She couldn't stop it now. She'd even helped him do it.

She reined Maureen to the right, back up the bank and along a trail that led toward the old homestead. She had always been able to think better there.

Still excited by the run, Maureen pranced and blew through her nostrils as they navigated the trail. Her gyrations startled a family of quail—mother, father and six little babies the size and shape of golf balls. As the parents herded their charges to safety in the underbrush, Freddy's heart wrenched with a new wave of pain. With a cry of anguish, she faced the death of dreams she hadn't even known she'd had until she saw the quail. Ry had awakened urges for a family of her own, children to teach in the ways of the ranch, to instruct in the legacy of the True Love.

"The place *is* cursed!" she shouted, causing Maureen to throw back her head in alarm. "And I'm a fool for trying to hold on," she said, gazing sightlessly at the trail ahead as she quieted her horse.

Maureen picked her way without guidance along the familiar trail she'd taken countless times with her mistress. Eventually, she halted in the clearing across from the ruins of the small adobe homestead. Freddy roused herself and dismounted, letting the reins drop to the ground so Maureen was free to graze.

As Freddy approached the crumbling adobe building, a green-collared lizard scurried across her path. She checked for spiders and scorpions before sitting on a portion of the ruined wall shaded by a large palo verde.

Taking off her hat, she ran the back of her sleeve across her face and sighed. Apparently, Ry and his partners only wanted the land the True Love occupied, not the ranch itself. She'd feared the dangers of a failed love affair, but this was worse, so much worse. She'd vowed to stay on the ranch until she was tossed off, but she couldn't imagine continuing as foreman knowing that Ry and his co-owners would sell to the first big developer who came along. Leigh might choose to stay on for a while, and Belinda might have no choice, considering Dexter's needs.

Dexter. Freddy's hands closed into fists and she longed to punch Ry in the face. Had he considered what destroying the ranch would do to Dexter? The old man would be dead within a year. And Duane. Where would he keep his precious herd now? He'd planned to use what money he earned with that herd to send his kids to college. His life would be in shambles if the ranch disappeared.

How could Ry do this? Yet, to be fair, she had to admit he'd never promised to preserve the ranch, only to buy it. She'd been blinded by lust into believing he had only the best of intentions toward her and the True Love. And he'd taken advantage of that attraction. God, how she hated him for that.

She gazed out at the desert—the prickly pear decorated in yellow, blossoms wide open, drinking in the afternoon sun. She'd opened herself like that for Ry, thinking to sun herself in his warmth. And she'd been burned.

She thought of Clara Singleton, a woman who'd known how to survive, how to give sexual favors without surrendering her heart, until she found a man like Thaddeus, who offered true love. Then Clara had reaped her reward, perhaps sitting near this very spot and admiring the cactus flowers. She must have appreciated the triumph of a cactus flower, beauty thriving amid harsh conditions, like Clara herself. Clara would most likely have pointed a 30-30 at a land grabber like Ry and ordered him off her spread.

Freddy's jaw clenched. So what was she doing? Meekly handing in her resignation and scuttling away? Giving up?

No, by God!

Freddy leaped to her feet and slapped her hat on her head. This homestead was a proven historical site, and somebody might give Mr. McGuinnes and his partners a really hard time about destroying it. And what about the John Wayne Room? What about the other famous people, some still alive, who had stayed there? There might be enough public sentiment attached to the entire ranch to hold up his development plans for years!

"We'll fight him all the way, Clara," she muttered, glancing at the old house. "You and I."

As she started toward Maureen, a rumble of thunder sounded in the distance. She glanced up into the cloudless sky. Probably a squadron of fighter jets from the air base, she thought, continuing toward her horse.

The rumble grew louder, and Maureen's head came up.

"What is it, girl?" Freddy asked, reaching for the mare's bridle.

Uncharacteristically, Maureen jerked her head away from Freddy's outstretched hand.

"Hey, it's probably a bunch of helicopters on maneuvers," Freddy said, following her uneasy horse. "It's probably—"

A Hereford crashed through the brush and headed straight for Maureen. The horse bolted just as another cow thundered past, and the ground began to shake.

"Maureen!" Freddy cried, running after the horse. But Maureen was gone, plunging wildly down the trail away from the stampeding herd. A heifer bumped Freddy from behind, almost sending her to the ground. She scrambled erect as a powerful shoulder brushed against her and spun her around to face a wall of russet-and-white faces surging toward her.

She lost a precious second as she stood paralyzed. Then she turned and ran for the edge of the clearing, grabbing a branch of the first mesquite she reached. Thorns bit into her palms as she braced a foot in the crotch of the tree and hauled herself up, losing her hat in the process. Just as she got her other foot off the ground, the first wave rushed past, shaking the trunk and rattling the branches. Her hands slipped, and she tightened her grip despite the thorns. Blood trickled down her wrist and soaked into the cuffs of her shirt.

She hauled herself higher, praying the tree was strong enough to hold her weight. A branch cracked but didn't fall as the cattle surged beneath her. Then the massed animals began banging into the trunk, jolting her with each impact.

Slowly, the tree began to lean.

"Help!" she shouted, knowing it was no use, knowing she was absolutely alone. But she shouted, anyway. "Help me! Please help me!"

"Freddy!"

Someone was there. She squinted through the dust as the tree leaned closer to the trampling herd. "Over here!"

Then she saw him, riding low over Red Devil's neck as the big horse plowed through the river of cattle. No, it should not be Ry. He wasn't a good enough rider to make it through a stampede. He would die trying to save her. "Go back!" she screamed. "I'll make it!"

She glimpsed the grim set of his mouth. He was coming for her. Her heart swelled in response to this show of courage. Foolish, foolish courage. *Oh, Ry! Please go back*, she begged silently, knowing it was no use. If she allowed him to pick her off the tree, as he obviously intended, they'd probably both fall under the churning hooves and be killed. But if she held back, he'd probably fall off trying to reach her and then they'd both die. A no-win situation.

He veered toward the tree, his arm extended. She poised herself for the pickup.

"Now!" he shouted, grabbing her by the belt.

She landed facedown across the front of his saddle, the impact knocking the air from her lungs. She stared straight into the wild eyes of a Hereford running beside Red Devil as she started to slip forward headfirst into the herd.

"No, dammit!" Ry shouted, jerking her back by her belt. "No!"

Gradually, Red Devil's pace slowed. The herd thinned, until Ry was able to rein the horse in. Red Devil stood snorting and shaking as Ry hauled Freddy upright and settled her facing him, her thighs resting across his.

Freddy gasped for breath. Ry's face was a mask of dust, and his chest heaved. He picked up one of her blood-encrusted hands and examined her palm. Then he placed a soft kiss there.

Tears welled in her eyes, and she was about to blubber out her gratitude, when she recalled why she'd ridden out here in the first place. Taking an unsteady breath, she lifted her chin and looked him square in the eye. "I hate your guts," she said.

"I know." He smiled.

"Furthermore, you're not getting away with this, you and your pack of thieves from the big city. I'm fighting you every inch of the way, buster. You haven't seen the last of Freddy Singleton!"

His smile widened.

"What are you doing, sitting there grinning like an idiot? Don't you realize what I'm saying? This is war!"

"I wouldn't expect anything less from you."

"So what's the big smile for, mister?"

"You're alive."

She stared at him, then cleared her throat. "Thank you for saving my life," she said stiffly.

"No thanks necessary. You did me a favor."

"I beg your pardon?"

He reined Red Devil in a circle and started toward the homestead. She was forced to grab hold of his waist to keep from falling off. Even worse, the movement of the horse, balanced as she was up against Ry's crotch, awakened some potent memories she would rather forget.

He held her gently with one arm around her waist, his chin hovering just above the crown of her head. "You see, Freddy, I came to Arizona feeling like a failure. Maybe I'd done well in the paper world of stocks and bonds, but I had no confidence I could make it in the nitty-gritty of real life. Deep down I was afraid that if I'd been faced with those punks who killed Linda, I might not have known what to do. It sounds corny, but my manhood had never been tested."

Ry was a lot harder to hate up close like this, she thought. She found herself hugging him tighter, and then she had to remember to relax her arms and back away as much as possible in this confining position.

"I think that's part of what buying this ranch was all about," he continued. "I wanted to come out here and test myself."

That statement helped renew her fury. "So we were a proving ground for you? How nice. Now you can turn the True Love into a suburban housing development because it's served your purpose."

He tightened his grip around her waist. "We need to talk about that."

"I'm not much in the mood for talking. I think I'd rather cut your heart out."

He sighed. "You may get your chance at that, too. But I—" He paused and pulled back on Red Devil's reins. "My God."

"What?" Glancing up, she saw him staring over Red Devil's head. She swiveled to follow the direction of his gaze, and her breath became trapped in her lungs.

Where the little homestead had once stood as a silent tribute to Clara and Thaddeus Singleton, nothing remained but a pile of rubble. Only the concrete slab had survived in one piece. A lump rising in her throat, Freddy held on to Ry as she wiggled her way out of the saddle and down to the ground. Slowly, she approached the trampled ruins as tears made tracks through the dust caking her face.

She leaned over, picked up a piece of an adobe brick and held the fragment tight in her fist as she imagined Thaddeus building the wooden forms for the adobe, hauling the sand, mixing the straw and the mud. Brick by brick he'd forged his place in the wilderness, built it for his beloved Clara. Freddy searched the debris for the lintel and found it smashed beyond repair. The heart with an arrow through it was in two pieces.

She picked them up and tried to fit them together, putting a splinter through her finger for her efforts. She'd always meant to have the site stabilized, meant to erect some barrier around it. Now it was too late. The home Thaddeus had built, the home Clara had risked her life fighting for, was gone.

"I'm sorry." Ry put an arm around her shoulders.

She wrenched away and whirled to face him. "How *dare* you say you're sorry? You want to bulldoze the whole place someday!"

Agony was etched on his face. "No, I don't."

"Really?" She saw him through a red film of rage. "Then where were you planning to put the subdivision? What about the golf course? Now I know why you were so interested in the water supply and landscaping. You, you *rapist!*"

He stepped forward and grabbed her. "Listen to me!"

"No!" She tried to twist away and the two pieces of wood fell from her grasp.

"Yes! I meant to do those things when I came here. I admit it! But I've changed, Freddy. You've changed me. Just now, I risked my life to save yours. And I succeeded." He gave her a little shake. "I succeeded! Do you understand how that makes me feel?"

"No," she said tightly.

His touch gentled. "For the first time in my life, I feel like a man. You gave me that. You and the True Love." He released her. "I don't want it to disappear any more than you do."

She stepped away from him, away from the seductive pull of his touch. "Then let Eb Whitlock buy it."

His eyes narrowed. "I can't do that."

"Why not?"

"Something's going on around here. I'm not convinced all the so-called accidents are accidents."

Even in the heat, she felt a chill run over her. "You think somebody's sabotaging the ranch?"

"Maybe. And Whitlock's one of my candidates."

"Oh, for heaven's sake! That thing with the petroleum drums was a case of bad memory."

"It could have been, but he seemed pretty focused to me. And then there's the question of Duane."

"Duane?"

"Did you see whose brand was on those cattle?"

She tried to remember, but the only thing that surfaced was a mass of heaving bodies with the power to kill her. "No, I didn't."

"I didn't either until the last two ran by me. They both carried the D-Bar on their left hip, Freddy."

"My God, Duane will be furious that his cattle got out and stampeded like that."

"Unless he stampeded them."

"What? You *are* paranoid, Ry McGuinnes!"

"Am I? When I got to the corrals, Duane was on the phone, and I think he was talking to Leigh. We can assume Leigh told him about the subdivision thing. When saddled up, he came out and asked where I was headed, and I told him over by the old homestead."

She gasped. "Just what are you implying?"

"You're the one who said Duane would do anything to protect his own. He could have figured you could handle yourself in a stampede if you happened to be around, but he may have reckoned I might not."

"No." She shook her head. "You're definitely wrong about this."

"Then what's the explanation for all the accidents? The True Love curse?"

"I'd accept that before I'd accuse anyone I've known and trusted most of my life."

He sighed. "I can understand that, but deep in your heart you know something's wrong around here, and you'll have to agree that several people have a motive for devaluing the property with these accidents. Besides, you don't strike me as the superstitious type."

"I refuse to be the suspicious type, either."

"Not even when you almost died?"

Freddy shoved her hands in the back pockets of her jeans and gazed down at the ground. A short distance away was the tree she'd climbed. It lay broken at the base, toppled over, its leaves and branches crushed. Nearby was a flat, grayish blob that was probably what remained of her hat. She shivered. Was it possible that someone was sabotaging her beloved ranch? If so, she needed an ally she could trust. She leveled a look at Ry. "You've said you don't want the ranch to disappear, but

you haven't said you'll work to save it, either. Looks lik
I don't have any good options."

He rubbed the back of his neck. "It's not an easy sit
uation. I can't buy it alone, and I've promised both part
ners we'll sell to developers and make a huge profit
That's why they're coming in with me."

Freddy's first reaction was despair. But she took a deep
breath and thought about the way Chase Lavette had
arrived today, decked out in boots, jeans and hat, al
dusty from a walk down the road. And hadn't Ry said
something about the third partner wanting to bring hi
son out to the True Love, to give him the experience o
being a cowboy? She studied Ry and compared him to
the man who had arrived in wing tips and tie.

"Are you sure that's why they're coming in with you
on this deal?" she asked. "To make big money?"

"Sure. Why else?"

"You didn't come here just for that. You've just con
fessed you wanted to test yourself."

"Yeah, but—"

"Ry, what if they're both like you, needing the True
Love for some personal reason but not quite ready to
admit it? So they use an acceptable excuse, such as mak
ing money, to be a part of a ranch, to live a different sor
of life."

The corner of his mouth tilted up. "Are you saying we
should get them out here and convert them to the idea of
keeping the ranch?"

"It seems to have worked with you."

"Yeah, but my case is a little different."

"How?"

The smile left his face and he regarded her with an in
tensity that sent a quiver through her. "I fell in love."

The earth seemed to drop away beneath her feet.

"Unfortunately" he said, "she doesn't feel the same way about me."

She gazed at him and remembered the emotion that had gripped her when she saw him riding through the stampede to save her. She'd been ready to give her life to save his. Even knowing how he'd deceived her about the ranch, she'd loved him enough to sacrifice herself. Even then. "Don't be too sure," she said unsteadily.

"Oh, I'm sure. You see, this lady's already given her heart away, and that love will always be her first priority. I'd have to accept second place. I'm not satisfied with that."

A pain sharper than she'd ever known knifed through her. "You would make me choose?" she whispered.

"Yes."

"Why?"

"Because I can't promise you that I'll be able to keep the ranch as it is. I can try, and we can hope my partners want to try, but the city could still grow around us, choking us out. We could lose zoning fights. We could go bankrupt. Even Thaddeus Singleton couldn't promise Clara that they'd always have the ranch. He could only promise his love. That's the one sure thing, Freddy." His hands clenched at his sides. "And it has to be enough."

A door swung open in her heart, a door rusty and unused.

"Let it be enough, Freddy," he murmured.

Joy shouldered its way through the door, filling the space where fear had reigned for so long. Happiness made it almost impossible to speak. But she had to say the words, had to give him what he sought. "I love you, Ry."

Intense emotion blazed in his eyes. Then he leaned down and picked up the two pieces of wood. "I think this can be fixed," he said gently. "It's more portable now," he added with a soft smile. "It can go wherever we go." He closed the distance between them. "Will you marry me, Frederica Singleton?"

"Yes."

He pulled her roughly into his arms and kissed her, dust and all. The pieces of wood in his hand imprinted themselves against her back as he tightened his hold. Clara would have approved of this moment, Freddy thought fleetingly. Then Ry's kiss deepened, and she abandoned thought altogether.

* * * * *

Watch for Chase's story in Temptation #559,
THE DRIFTER, *available in October wherever
Harlequin books are sold.*

HARLEQUIN

Temptation

COMING NEXT MONTH

#557 PASSION AND SCANDAL Candace Schuler
Bachelor Arms Book 9

Welcome to Bachelor Arms, a trendy L.A. apartment building, where you'll bump into colorful neighbors and hear gossip about the tenants. Gossip such as: What *really* happened in apartment 1-G years ago? Willow Ryan puts Steve Hart's investigative skills—and his passionate feelings for her—to the test when she decides to uncover the scandalous truth.

#558 KISS OF THE BEAST Mallory Rush
Secret Fantasies Book 10

Do you have a secret fantasy? Researcher Eva Campbell does. She's an expert on virtual reality, and in her computer she's created the perfect man. Except, her fantasy lover is much more real than she could *ever* imagine....

#559 THE DRIFTER Vicki Lewis Thompson
Urban Cowboys Book 2

A Stetson and spurs don't make a man a cowboy. But New York truck driver, Chase Lavette, could have been born on a ranch. And like most cowboys, he was a drifter who avoided any form of commitment. But then gorgeous Amanda Drake came to the True Love ranch, bringing with her the son Chase never knew he had!

#560 MAKE-BELIEVE HONEYMOON Kristine Rolofson

Jilted and jobless...but that was no reason *not* to go on her honeymoon Kate Stewart decided. London, England, was the homeplace of many of her fantasies: dashing lords and flirtatious ladies. Besides, Kate was beginning to realize she wasn't all that heartbroken! Especially after she met the dark and brooding Duke of Thornecrest....

AVAILABLE NOW:

#553 SEDUCED AND BETRAYED
Candace Schuler
Bachelor Arms Book 8

#554 STRANGER IN MY ARMS
Madeline Harper
Secret Fantasies Book 9

#555 THE TRAILBLAZER
Vicki Lewis Thompson
Urban Cowboys Book 1

#556 THE TEXAN
Janice Kaiser
Rebels & Rogues

Take 4 bestselling love stories FREE

Plus get a FREE surprise gift!

Harlequin Romance ®

AVAILABLE IN OCTOBER—A BRAND-NEW COVER DESIGN FOR HARLEQUIN ROMANCE

Harlequin Romance has a fresh new eye-catching cover.

We're bringing you an exciting new cover design, but Harlequin Romance is still committed to bringing you warm and contemporary love stories that are sure to touch your heart!

See how we've changed and look for these fabulous stories with a brand-new look:

#3379 Brides for Brothers
by Debbie Macomber
#3380 The Best Man
by Shannon Waverly
#3381 Once Burned
by Margaret Way
#3382 Legally Binding
by Jessica Hart

Available in October, wherever Harlequin books are sold.

Harlequin Romance ®—
Dare To Dream

URBAN COWBOYS

A Stetson and spurs don't make a man a cowboy.

Being a real cowboy means being able to tough it out on the ranch and on the range. Three Manhattan city slickers with something to prove meet that challenge…and succeed.

But are they man enough to handle the three wild western women who lasso their hearts?

Bestselling author Vicki Lewis Thompson will take you on the most exciting trail ride of your life with her fabulous new trilogy—Urban Cowboys.

THE TRAILBLAZER #555 (September 1995)

THE DRIFTER #559 (October 1995)

THE LAWMAN #563 (November 1995)

HARLEQUIN® *Temptation*

HARLEQUIN®

Temptation

Secret Fantasies

Do you have a secret fantasy?

Researcher Eva Campbell does. She's an expert on
virtual reality and in her computer she's created the
perfect man. Except her fantasy lover is much more
real than she could ever imagine.... Experience
love with the ideal man in Mallory Rush's #558
KISS OF THE BEAST, available in October.

Everybody has a secret fantasy. And you'll find them
all in Temptation's exciting new yearlong miniseries,
Secret Fantasies. Throughout 1995 one book each
month focuses on the hero or heroine's innermost
romantic desires....

Become a
$\mathcal{P}$rivileged $\mathcal{W}$oman,
$\mathcal{Y}$ou'll be entitled to all these $\mathcal{F}$ree $\mathcal{B}$enefits.
And $\mathcal{F}$ree $\mathcal{G}$ifts, too.

To thank you for buying our books, we've designed an exclusive FREE program called *PAGES & PRIVILEGES*™. You can enroll with just one Proof of Purchase, and get the kind of luxuries that, until now, you could only read about.

$\mathcal{B}$IG HOTEL DISCOUNTS

A privileged woman stays in the finest hotels. And so can you—at up to 60% off! Imagine standing in a hotel check-in line and watching as the guest in front of you pays $150 for the same room that's only costing you $60. Your *Pages & Privileges* discounts are good at Sheraton, Marriott, Best Western, Hyatt and thousands of other fine hotels all over the U.S., Canada and Europe.

$\mathcal{F}$REE DISCOUNT TRAVEL SERVICE

A privileged woman is always jetting to romantic places.

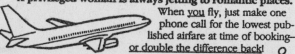

When <u>you</u> fly, just make one phone call for the lowest published airfare at time of booking— <u>or double the difference back!</u>

PLUS—you'll get a $25 voucher to use the first time you book a flight AND <u>5% cash back on every ticket you buy thereafter through the travel service!</u>

PROOF OF PURCHASE

Offer expires October 31, 1996

HT-PP57